Smoking Holt

A Tryst Island Erotic Romance

SABRINA YORK

ISBN-13: 978-0-9891577-7-3

DEDICATION

This book is dedicated to Desiree Holt, Gina Lamm and Alexandra Cross. When you read the book, you'll know why, if you don't already.

ACKNOWLEDGMENTS

First of all, thanks to my amazing beta readers, Charmaine Arredondo, Carmen Cook, Shelly Estes and Hollie Reith. My deepest appreciation to Wicked Smart Designs for a rocking cover, and to Monica Britt for helping me whip this novella into shape.

Thank you so much to my dear writerly friends for your support: Avery Aster, Sidney Bristol, Cerise de Land, Delilah Devlin, Tina Donahue, Kate Hill, Desiree Holt, Gina Lamm and Kate Richards. And to Crystal Biby, Dee Thomas, Angie Lane, Laurie Peterson, Regina Ross and Ronlyn Howe, I adore you.

To all my friends in the Greater Seattle Romance Writers of America, Passionate Ink and Rose City Romance Writers groups, thank you for all your support and encouragement.

CHAPTER ONE

It was raining. The patter of the raindrops pounded a relentless tattoo on the umbrella over her head, but Bella didn't care.

It suited her mood.

The night was dark, damp. She could hear the restless crash of the waves on the beach, but couldn't see anything beyond the veil of mist. Thunder rumbled in the distance, as though the gods wanted to grumble a complaint about the way life was turning out, but lacked the inspiration to give it full force.

Yeah. The weather suited her mood perfectly. Hunkering deeper into the patio chair, she took another deep draw on her cigarette.

She hated the taste, the smell, the burn in her throat, but there was a deep satisfaction in the action. Watching the embers flare. Seeing the paper darken and curl and then waft away in a drift of smoke. As though she could burn away all the petty annoyances, all the disappointments, all the failures of her life.

No one knew she still smoked. Not her sister Kristi, not her mom, none of her friends. That was part of the thrill, she supposed.

Her secret rebellion.

She reached for the tumbler of whiskey—her not-so-secret rebellion— and tipped it back. Then filled it again. A warm glow infused her as the spirit slid smoothly into her veins.

God, she needed this.

Time to herself. Time to smoke and drink with no one watching or judging or, for fuck's sake, nagging.

She'd come to the beach house she shared with her friends two days early, breaking the rules and not signing in on their online calendar. Because, fuck it. She needed to get away. So after a dismal meeting with her distributor, picking up some new sample items, she headed straight for the ferry, a dark cloud of doom swirling around her.

Her business was struggling; bills were piling up. Her love life was miserable. That last date with Jeremy had been a disaster of shit-storm proportions. And to top it all off, everything seemed to be going just swimmingly for Kristi.

Bella had no right to be jealous of her older sister, who had finally connected with the man of her dreams—the guy she'd been in love with since fucking college. But damn it, it pissed her off. Everything always seemed to work out for Kristi. All she had to do was show up, flash that bright smile and the universe laid everything right at her feet.

Bella had to work, slave, fight for everything. Every goddamn little thing.

Kristi's coffee bar was thriving. Somehow she and Lucy had done everything right, setting up shop in Montlake, the heart of computer nerd country and a short hop from the bustling University of Washington. On a bad day there were lines out the door. Bella's boutique was lucky to get ten customers a day. Granted, she had a more select clientele, but if she didn't find a way to drive more customers to her business, it was going to have to close. And then what would she do?

Go sling Americanos for her sister?

How mortifying would that be?

And how awful would it be to let Abel and Mirriam go? Mirriam had two kids. She needed this job. And she was damn good at it.

Bella scrubbed her eyes with the heel of her palm, as though that could make her seething thoughts settle. But they didn't. Couldn't.

Like a heat seeking missile, they settled on the other frustration burning a hole in her gut. Her love life.

She snorted. Love life. Right.

A couple of dates with a guy, who only wanted to "tap that" as he put it, did not a love life make. She should have known Jeremy was a douche nozzle. He had all the hallmark tags. Hell, he waved red flags like a semaphore expert.

But she was no expert in reading the signs. Clearly.

She'd allowed him to flirt with her, then woo her and then finally seduce her.

She'd thought there'd been something there, a flicker of attraction at least. Turned out it was only a notch on a bedpost. A bedpost scarred with other notches.

And on top of all of that, despite her determined vegan dieting, she'd gained another pound. Honestly. One bacon bender had wiped away all her hard work. Like a sandcastle obliterated by a tsunami. Of bacon.

Kristi could eat like there was no tomorrow and still somehow seemed to be curvy, not plump. It wasn't fair. It wasn't fair at all.

Bella stubbed out her cigarette and lit another. Not that she was chain smoking. She wasn't. She just knew once everyone else showed up for the weekend, she'd be back to chewing nicotine gum. It was now or never.

The house would be full this weekend, if everyone who signed in showed up. There would be no opportunity to sneak off for a smoke.

Why that made a sizzle of exasperation curl through her gut, she didn't know. It had nothing to do with the fact *he* was coming. Hell, she didn't even think about Holt Lamm anymore. She had purged him from her mind completely. Completely.

And she wasn't addicted.

Smoking was a rebellion, not a habit.

She could quit anytime she wanted to.

She just didn't want to.

But she didn't want anyone else to know. And didn't want to think on why. Surely she didn't care what they thought of her.

Bella Cross was a freaking rebel. Everyone knew it. Her tattoos and piercings screamed it. She was the daughter of a minister. She owned a sex shoppe. Surely that illustrated her bone-deep mutinous nature.

Tipping back her second drink, she poured another, ignoring the wobble of her hand. It was her intention to get shit-faced tonight. Maybe then she could forget about—

No! She wasn't thinking about him. She wasn't.

God damn Holt anyway. Why did he have to be so fucking good looking? He was tall and muscular and solid. His hair and eyes were dark, his hair long and wild. Just the way she liked it. And he simmered with repressed sexuality.

Well, maybe not so repressed.

Yeah. That was what pissed her off. The fact that he fucked anything in a skirt—tied it down and fucked it—but he wouldn't even look at her sideways. He never flirted with her. Not the way he flirted with Emily. And Kaitlin. And, for fuck's sake, Kristi.

It wasn't fair. It just wasn't fair.

Everyone wanted Kristi. Every guy she'd ever even liked or dated or slept with just really wanted Kristi.

Shit.

She should just give up on men and become a nun.

Could nuns run sex shoppes?

Well hell. What did it matter? In six months she'd be broke. Her little shoppe would close.

She could be a nun then.

Probably better smoke all she could now.

She was in the process of lighting another cigarette, preparing for impending nunnery, when a light flared behind her.

3

Crap! No one was supposed to be here until Friday!

Bella whipped around and glared into the living room behind her. And her heart froze in her throat. A tall, dark form emerged from the shadows in the hall. Irritation—and something else entirely—crawled through her belly.

As though she had conjured him from her dismal ruminations, Holt Lamm had arrived on Tryst Island.

He saw her and his steps slowed. He dropped his duffel onto a chair and headed for the slider.

Bella glanced at the cigarette she held. The pack on the table. The saucer filled with butts. Oh, sure, she could scramble and try to hide it all, but she would fail. And, according to the whiskey swimming through her veins, she didn't give a shit if he knew or not.

She was a fucking rebel. And if he didn't like it, he could go fuck himself.

Hell, he was probably the only person on the planet, aside from herself, he *hadn't* fucked.

She snorted at her own inebriated humor.

That was half the fun of being drunk. Your thoughts seem clever for once.

The door slid open and Holt stepped out onto the deck. Bella turned to study the gloomy marine layer and sucked in another draw on her cigarette, deliberately ignoring him.

Which was stupid.

But necessary.

He sat in the patio chair by her side and shook the raindrops from his head.

She didn't look. Didn't need to. She knew what his long locks looked like wet. And dry. And pulled back. And flowing freely. She'd memorized every aspect of his being.

The heat rolling off him in waves was probably pure imagination on her part. Nobody could be that hot and not just burst into flames.

"Bella." His voice was a low rumble, which she found provoking. Probably because of the hint of rebuke threaded through the word. Still, the sound of her name on those lips made her restless. Itchy.

"Holt." This, she blew out in a puff of smoke. The breeze caught it, danced it away. Would that she could dance away as well.

The thought of spending the next two days alone with him was torture. Absolute torture. Every time she so much as glanced at him, a ping of pain hummed through her soul.

He leaned back in his chair, stretched his long legs out under the glass table and threaded his fingers over his belly. Her gaze fixated on his boots. Why did he have to be wearing boots? And leathers?

The fact that he rode his Harley almost everywhere was just one more thing that annoyed the shit out of her. Surely it wasn't because he was a much more authentic rebel than she.

"No one's supposed to be here until Friday." Okay. She probably didn't need to snap like that, but goddamn it anyway. Why was he here?

He picked up the whiskey bottle, checked the level and then took a swig. "I finished my project early. Decided to take the rest of the week off."

Yeah. Someone else with a thriving business. Someone else with an enormously successful career. She grunted and muttered under her breath, "Must be nice."

"And why are you here on a Wednesday?"

As if it was any of his business. She glared at him. "Slow week." Fuck. Every week was a slow week. Abel and Marianne had agreed to cover the store. With so few customers, merchandise was gathering dust on the shelves. Why not come here and lick her wounds in private?

But it wasn't private.

Not now.

If she weren't so drunk, and if the last ferry hadn't already sailed, she would just go home now. She tipped back her glass and drained it, though it was still half full. Then she attempted to wrestle the bottle from him. He didn't seem to want to release it.

"Haven't you had enough?" he asked.

The idiot.

She snarled at him. No words. Just a snarl. He let the bottle go with a shrug, raising his hands in the air and she filled her glass. To the fucking brim.

"I didn't know you still smoked."

Yeah. There it was. Finally. She'd been waiting for that bomb to drop.

She lit another cigarette, although there was one already burning, and glared at him through the billow of smoke. He was so annoying with that chiseled jaw, those full, lush lips and slumberous, heavy-lidded eyes. That goddamned five-o'clock shadow drove her fucking crazy.

"Does Kristi know?"

Fury and frustration and hunger roiled in her chest. Why couldn't he ever, like once, think about her? Why was it always about Kristi? "Fuck you, Holt. I don't answer to anyone."

He laughed, which pissed her off even more. "No. You don't. Do you?"

What the fuck was that supposed to mean?

She opened her mouth to ask, but before she could, he added, "You always did march to the beat of another drummer."

Something in his tone, something that definitely wasn't scorn, snagged her attention. Was she just drunk, or had that been a tinge of…admiration? She narrowed her eyes and studied him. "What is that supposed to mean?"

Though she voiced her thought, the question lacked her trademark bitterness. The prospect of Holt having even a smidgen of respect for her was tantalizing. Dangerous, perhaps, but tantalizing.

He took another drink from the bottle and shrugged. "You just live your life the way you want. Say what needs to be said. You don't give a shit what other people think."

"I give a shit." But this, she mumbled. There was a distinct difference between not giving a shit and letting people think you didn't give a shit. She'd made an art of the latter. The scary truth was, she probably cared too much. Sometimes it hurt, how much she cared.

She turned away, away from his too-observant, simmering gaze, away from his heat, and stared out into the night. A shiver took her. The evening was cold and damp. She should probably go inside.

Instead, she lit another cigarette.

He snorted a laugh.

"What?" she snapped.

"You already have two going." She flicked a glance at her impromptu ashtray. Yup, sure enough, there were two cigarettes already burning.

She shrugged and forced a devil-may-care tone. "What can I say? I have an oral fixation."

He went still at her side, prompting her to look in his direction. The fire in his eyes seared her.

"What?" Again, a snap. God, he was irritating.

He licked his lips as though he wanted to say something, but the words were stuck in his throat.

"What?"

A tiny smile quirked on his handsome face. "If you didn't hate my guts so much, I'd be tempted to give you something else to fixate on."

Her heart thudded painfully. And not just at the sudden, scalding image of her lips wrapped around Holt's cock. She fiddled with her lighter. "I-I don't hate your guts."

"Really?" He took another swig of whiskey. And then another. "You could have fooled me. You called me a—what was it again?—a douche nozzle?"

"You were acting like a douche nozzle. I mean, really. What decent man dates five women at once?"

"They all knew the score. There was no agreement of monogamy. And what else am I? A peckerwood. A horndog." His voice dropped an octave. "A degenerate."

A red tide crawled up her neck. Yeah. She'd said all those things. But she hadn't meant them. Not really.

"If the shoe fits…"

"But it wasn't what you said…it was how you said it. As though it tasted bad."

She didn't like the wounded expression on his face, or the throb in this tone. Had her careless words really cut that deep? She didn't like the way that made her feel at all.

So she went on the defensive.

"You're the one who can't stand me." She didn't know why she said that out loud. Or why the words seemed to wrench from the very depths of her soul.

Oh. Wait. She did know why she said it.

The whiskey.

But, it was the truth. Whenever he glanced at her, the tiny lines around his mouth would tighten and his attention would slide away. Toward Kristi, or some other female. Whenever he wandered into a room and saw her there alone he would just veer off in another direction. And when he spoke to her, whenever he deigned to address her directly, his words were curt and clipped.

No. He couldn't stand her. It was hardly a secret.

And it pissed her off.

She shot a glower at him and something froze in her chest. Probably her heart. Or her anger. Or her heart. Because he wasn't looking at her with apathy or revulsion or some fake contrition.

He looked stunned. "Where did you get the idea I can't stand you?"

"Gee, I don't know, Holt." She stubbed out her cigarette. And then the other two. "Maybe the way you treat me like I have a disease?"

"I do not."

"All right. Warts then." She rubbed the annoying prickle at the corner of her lids. She wasn't going to cry. She wasn't.

"Bella—"

"It's okay, Holt. I get it. I'm hardly your type. But could you at least—"

"You're exactly my type." He said it softly enough, but she heard it. The words percolated through her booze-pickled brain.

"What did you say?"

He sat back, eyes glowing. "You heard me."

They stared at each other in silence as the rain pattered on the big umbrella and then dripped onto the deck in fat splats. Tension and desire crackled between them. It became almost too intense to bear.

Bella fumbled for her pack of cigarettes, but Holt covered her hand with his. "No. No more," he said. "Not tonight. Fixate on this instead." And he leaned forward and lowered his head.

.

CHAPTER TWO

Holt couldn't believe it. She was holding still as he came in for a kiss. A kiss he'd been fantasizing about for months.

And who wouldn't fantasize about kissing Bella? She was drop-dead gorgeous. Just looking at her made his mouth water. His cock hard. He could barely contemplate more. Much less make an attempt.

Maybe it was the whiskey he'd guzzled on an empty stomach or maybe it was the desolation surrounding her like a cloak. Or maybe it was the burn of repressed need rising up within him. But somewhere during their awkward, confrontational exchange—and they were always awkward and confrontational—a sudden resolve had washed over him. A determination to change things between them.

It had been like this for far too long. And he had no idea why.

Holt threaded his fingers in Bella's silky hair and cupped her nape, pulled her closer. Her lips parted and her tongue peeped out as he approached. Desire raged through him.

He'd wanted her, ached for a taste of her for so long, he could barely breathe, now that he'd finally dredged up the courage.

But breathing was overrated.

His lips touched hers. Her scent, her essence, filled his mouth and he groaned. She tasted like ambrosia.

Okay. There was a hint of whiskey and a trace of menthol, but he could overlook that. For the moment. Because—shit—her lips moved beneath his. And not a murmur of protest or outrage or fury or any of the other responses he might have expected in the unlikely event he might grab her and suddenly kiss her with no warning.

No. She was exploring, tasting, sipping him like a woman long denied.

He tipped his head to the side and deepened the kiss. His gut clenched when she opened for him, gave him better access. And then—yeah, his cock sprang to attention—she sank her claws into his shoulder and tugged him closer.

She nipped him. Just a gentle nip to his lower lip. And his vision went red.

He didn't mean to growl.

He didn't mean to go all feral and wrench her chair around in a metallic squeal of protest.

He didn't mean to scoop her up into his arms and hold her luscious form hard against his body while he consumed her. Bracing her on the table, using the umbrella pole for leverage, he grasped her buttocks and positioned her over his crotch and rubbed, dry humping her like a lust-crazed beast. The ashtray and the whiskey bottle fell onto the deck as he jostled the table in his frenzy to feel her fully against him. He ignored them. Ignored them and rubbed his cock against the damp heat of her core.

Sure, it was through two layers of jeans, but it was closer than he'd ever been to heaven in his life.

He had to revise that thought a moment later when Bella, who was, unbelievably, undulating against his cock and grunting and moaning, tossed back her hair and stared at him. The fire in her eyes stole his breath.

"Holt," she whispered through clenched teeth. "God, yes, Holt."

Now *that* was the closest he'd ever been to heaven.

That look, those words. Jesus. A dream come true.

Why the hell hadn't he grabbed her and kissed her with no warning before?

Because he'd thought, deep in his heart, she'd push him away. Maybe slap him. Certainly dress him down. Never in his wildest imagination had he expected this. Well, maybe in his wildest fantasies. Maybe in all his fantasies.

But he'd never thought it would really happen.

He held her close, cupping the small of her back, and nibbled his way over her cheek and along her jaw to suck on her earlobe. She went crazy, huffing and moaning and fisting—*fucking fisting*—his hair.

He'd never been into hair pulling, at least having his hair pulled, but something about her rough and riotous response to his nips and laves made the fire in his belly flare. He responded in kind, twining his fingers in the skeins of her hair, holding her still at just the right angle as he explored the exquisite column of her neck.

He cradled her breast. Squeezed. He couldn't resist. God. She was soft. Full. Delicious. He longed to yank off her shirt, rip off her bra, expose those tremendous globes to his hungry sight.

He wanted her naked. He wanted in her. Now.

A fury of passion enflamed him. A passion that could not be quenched—

He stilled as a cold finger traced its way down his back and, unerringly, found its way to the crease of his ass. And another. And another. And then the finger became an icy rivulet.

He glanced up to see that, during their tumult, the umbrella had tipped and was now funneling a stream of cold water right onto him.

Goddamn rain.

Whatever happened now, it wasn't going to happen here.

He didn't want to chance jostling her from this receptive mood so without asking he lifted Bella into his arms and carried her into the house. He nuzzled her neck as he made this transition, because it seemed to keep her preoccupied. And hell, he really liked her response.

Who knew she would be such a tigress?

Well, he'd known.

He'd suspected anyway.

Every conversation, every interaction with Bella was like a battle for domination. It stood to reason making love with her would be the same. And while there was nothing Holt enjoyed more than exerting domination over a willing woman, the prospect of winning it, from Bella, appealed much much more.

He sat in the first chair he came to, settled her across his lap and kissed her again. This time he took her mouth slowly, savoring her, rubbing his lips gently over hers before delving deeper with his tongue.

He nearly lost his load when she sucked on him, mimicking another act he'd fantasized about. A lot.

God, he bet she gave great head.

She approached everything in life with passion. Most of the time her passion was misdirected and exasperating, but when she applied herself to something, it was a whole-hearted effort.

He repositioned her as the pressure in his cock became excruciating. She wiggled back and he groaned. "Jesus, Bella."

Yeah. He shouldn't have spoken. Words could shatter the spell.

She pulled away and gazed at him, her eyes luminous and damp. "Oh my God," she said. "What are we doing?" She wriggled against him in an attempt to escape. He did not allow it.

"I should think that was obvious."

"Seriously Holt. Seriously?" She wriggled again. He tightened his hold. A part of him ached at the fact she wanted to slip away. Another part of him really enjoyed the wriggling.

"I'm dead serious, Bella."

"This isn't a good idea." She stopped resisting, but her chest rose and fell a bit too rapidly, indicating her internal distress. "You? Me? Like this?"

"Why not? That was a phenomenal first kiss. Can you imagine what the rest of it could be like?"

She stilled and stared at him. Her lips worked as she thought through the scenario. And goddamn, it was hot watching her think that through. When he saw that telltale flicker, when rational thought began to wedge its way in, he decided to push it.

Why the fuck not?

She'd been wild and inflamed in his arms. Clearly she felt something other than disgust for him. If there was even so much as a hint of attraction lurking in her breast, he would find it. Stroke it. Seduce it.

He could not let this go.

Not now that he'd tasted her.

"I want to fuck you, Bella." This he whispered, caressing her breast and thumbing a nipple. It was hard, that nipple. Swollen and tender. "I want to make love to you. I want to make you come. I want you screaming in pleasure. Clenching my cock with your cunt." When she didn't pull away, when her eyes widened and her beautiful lips parted and she whimpered a little in her throat, he tightened his hold on that tender crest.

"But I'm not... You can't... I don't..."

"Hush."

God preserve him from thinking women. He didn't want her thinking. Didn't need her thinking. Couldn't bear to lose the ground he'd gained.

He dipped his head and put his mouth around her other nipple, manipulating one in his tight grasp while he sucked on the other through her shirt. This time when she wriggled, it was to get closer, to urge him on. She probably didn't even realize her sharp nails were scoring his skull.

He didn't give a shit. She could draw blood if she wanted to. As long and she let him continue.

To that end, he skated his other hand down her flank and over her thigh. And then, ever so smoothly, between her legs. She winced as he brushed against that heated crease. He pressed harder, imagining he felt a dampness pooling there.

Hunger churned in his gut. His pulse pounded in his cock. He flicked open the snap of her jeans and stroked her soft belly, then slipped beneath the band of her panties.

Thunder roared in his ears as he found her nest. Yeah, it was a tight fit, wedged into her jeans as he was, but a man needed to make the most of every situation. He covered her clit with three fingers and massaged her with tiny, restricted arcs as he relentlessly worked her nipples.

Her breathing devolved into gasps, and then hard pants. "Holt," she panted, grabbing hold of his ears. "Holt. Holt. Holt!"

He didn't need that gush of cream to tell him she'd come. Or the rigid spasms of her body. Or her assiduous grasp on his ears. The tone of her voice was plenty. It was a tone he'd never heard before, a low panicked hum, marking her complete loss of control.

God, he loved that tone.

He wanted to hear it again. And again.

Preferably with his cock buried deep in her body.

He liked making her lose control.

What he did not like was that she sprang from his lap almost as soon as she recovered herself. She took him at unawares, or he'd never have let her go.

She turned away from him, though he could see her clearly in the reflection of the windows, and fastened her jeans and rearranged her shirt. No matter how she rearranged that shirt, the wet spot where he had suckled her nipple as she came, the evidence of her passion, was still clearly visible.

She sucked in a deep breath. Then whirled around to face him.

His mood plummeted. Hell. He knew that look.

When she opened her mouth, he knew what she'd say.

"That shouldn't have happened."

The fuck.

The hell.

No way.

She was not going to deny this. He was not going to allow her to retreat back into that hard, impenetrable Bella-shell, the armor she wore to keep everyone and everything at bay.

He stood and faced her down, matching her stubbornness with his own brand. "Wrong." Her eyes flared. Her nostrils pinched as he countermanded her announcement. He stepped closer. "It should have happened a long, long time ago."

.

CHAPTER THREE

Bella stared at Holt. Just stared. It was all she could manage. Her body was still aquiver, weeping from his gentle touch, and aching for more, but her mind rebelled.

Her instinct for self-preservation screamed "No!"

He was a dangerous guy. Far more dangerous than any of the men she'd ever dated. Or slept with. And not just because of the depth of her seething attraction to him. Not just because she'd secretly wanted him for years.

She *knew him*, and knew him well. It was no secret, what he was into. And she wasn't his type. In a big way.

Not that she was strictly vanilla. She wasn't. A little kink could really spice up a relationship…or a date. But Holt was a hard-core Dom. He went to clubs. Tied women up for fun. Kept "pets."

There was no way she could ever be one of those women. No way.

The very thought horrified her.

She was a strong, independent woman. She stood on her own two feet. Answered to no one.

Needed no one.

She certainly didn't need him.

Wanting him—well, that was another issue entirely. She had always been drawn to him, even as she threw invectives at his tousled head. She would always fantasize about him. Always ache for him. Even when she was old and grey.

And single.

Living with her twenty cats.

But she would never be one of his women. She knew the kind of woman he craved.

She would never become that.

He stepped even closer and she stepped back, holding out a hand as though it could stave off his relentless advance. "This isn't going to work. Holt."

To her relief, he stopped just before he reached her, though he stood close. Close enough for her to feel the sizzle of his energy, the waves of his heat.

"Isn't it?" He quirked a brow. "It seemed to work just fine a moment ago. In fact, I didn't have to do too much to have you coming like a wildcat."

She frowned. "I did not come like a wildcat."

He lifted his hair, exposing the long, tanned column of his neck. She tried not to fixate on the long, silky locks, now that she knew how they felt sifting through her fingers. "Would you like to see my scars?" He chuckled. "I think you drew blood."

Before she could stop herself, she glanced down at her fingernails, just to check. No. No blood.

"Tell me you didn't like that Bella. Tell me you didn't enjoy any of that at all, and I'll drop this, right here and now."

She glared at him. Opened her mouth to do just that, but something stayed her tongue. Her soul howled in denial and the words, "I didn't enjoy that" just would not come out.

It was a lie and she knew it.

Instead, she turned her back on him. "That's not the point."

His chuckle rumbled through her and she realized he'd come up behind her. She winced as he set his hands on her shoulders and pulled her back against him. His warmth tempted her, but she refused to relax. She refused to lean in. Give an inch. "I think it's exactly the point." He eased her hair off her neck and set his mouth to her nape.

Ribbons of delight scoured her like a lash. She couldn't help tipping her head to the side, but only a little because she didn't want to encourage him. She didn't dare.

"I've wanted you for a long time Bella. Thought about you. Imagined kissing you. Holding you. Touching you like this." He cupped her breasts. Squeezed gently. Gently, yes, but her sensitized nipples still tightened.

His warm mouth traveled to the crook of her neck. She shivered. Sighed. "There's something between us. You can't deny it."

"I-I c-can."

He grunted a little laugh. She heard the thread of frustration in his tone, but something else as well. Something she didn't recognize. "I know you can, Bella, sweet. You can deny it until you're blue in the face. But your body knows the truth."

His fingers tightened over her nipples. Turned into a pinch. A tug. And her knees threatened to collapse. Her body liquefied. Dampness swelled between her legs. Her stupid clit thrummed in tandem with her thudding pulse.

"Damn it, Holt. It just wouldn't work between us. I... You... Shit." It was all she could manage, because he was wreaking havoc on her body and mind. He excelled at havoc. She wrenched away and whirled on him. "I won't be one of your...pets."

She tried not to spit the word, but that's how it came out.

"Is that what you think I want?"

"It's what you like, isn't it? To bully women? To boss them around and make them do what you want? I'm not like that Holt, in case you hadn't noticed—"

"I had noticed."

"I'm not some weak-willed bimbo tottering around naked in stilettos, wearing a collar and a leash and doing some man's fucking laundry."

He stared at her, his mouth slightly agape. When he finally spoke, his voice was rough. "A charming picture. Intriguing, I must admit...but I would never ask you to do my laundry."

The way his lips quirked, she knew he was teasing and it infuriated her. Because this was no joke. "Goddamn it, Holt. I'm serious." As serious as hell.

His mouth tightened. A muscle in his cheek bunched. "So am I. And for your information, my lifestyle isn't about bullying women. It isn't about bullying anyone. It's about two people exploring their sexuality from different angles. Experimenting with different roles. Finding where they meet and match and merge."

"You're a Dom, Holt."

"Yes. Predominantly. But I've had partners who weren't submissives."

"But you prefer submissive women."

"No. I prefer women who are open to exploration."

"You like to be the one in control."

His laugh, the sharp bark that it was, surprised her.

She frowned at him. "What?"

"One would think you'd know a little more about the lifestyle, considering the clientele you serve."

Bella's frown became a glower. "What the fuck is that supposed to mean?"

"I've been to your shop. I've seen your 'BDSM section'."

"Why do you say it like that?" With air quotes?

"It's hardly comprehensive."

Her lips flapped. "It's perfectly comprehensive. I ordered practically everything from the catalog."

He just snorted. "At any rate, it's pretty clear you don't understand a thing about the life, if you think it's about a man bullying a woman. The Dom is not the one in control," he said. "Not in a truly healthy D/s relationship. Not in my relationships. The sub calls the shots. Draws the lines. It's a partnership, Bella, where the sub controls everything."

She crossed her arms over her chest. "That is hard to believe."

"I'd be happy to give you a demonstration." The way he said it, with that quirk of his dark brow, the glint in his eyes, sent a ripple of exasperation—and something else—through her.

"Fuck you, Holt."

He grinned. "Okay."

Goddamn it. She wasn't sure which annoyed her more. His simmering sensuality or his goddamn teasing. Both were nearly irresistible. Against her will, her lips tweaked in a smile. He would take a smile as encouragement, she was certain of it.

Sure enough, he took that last, lethal step and yanked her into his arms, sealing them together. He was hot, hard, huge. She tipped up her chin and glared at him, opened her mouth to say something else, something pithy and snarky. Something that would drive him away and give her room to fucking breathe—

But he didn't give her time. No time to think of something pithy. No time to prepare. No time to shore up her defenses.

His mouth took hers. There was no other way to describe it. He covered her, smothered her, soaked her with his taste and his scent, suffused her with sensation. The rub of his lips over hers, the nibbles, the nips, the bold forays of his tongue, all scrambled her brain. His hands molded her ass, rubbing her against his body, dragging her groin over his. Somewhere in the back of her mind, she was aware that he was guiding her, moving her, walking her backwards in a relentless drive to crawl inside her.

And then she hit the wall.

Literally.

He backed her up against the wood paneling of the great room and pressed against her. His cock was like a stone. A fat, throbbing stone. Burning against the tender flesh of her belly.

A flash of pure, unadulterated lust whipped through her. Because he was hard. For her.

Oh sure, he'd probably be hard if he was mouth fucking Kristi here against the wood paneling. Or Emily. Or Lucy.

Or Lassie.

But this one was for her.

She knew she should push him away. As goddamn aggressive as he was, Holt would respect a "No" from a woman. But something deep within her recoiled at the prospect of ending this.

Not just yet.

It was too fucking thrilling.

A chance like this would never come again. Not in a million years.

She could fuck him tonight. Have a crazy, dirty, sweaty fuckfest and then tomorrow, blame it on the whiskey.

His lips released hers, but only so he could move to her neck, to work her, suckle her, nibble on the sensitive screaming skin there. Bella threw back her head so he had better access. She lifted her leg and wrapped it around his waist, plastering her slit against the monstrosity bulging at the juncture of his thighs.

"Shit," he growled, undulating against her. Delight washed through her in waves. She scored his scalp in a rake of need.

"You are not tying me up," she grunted.

He lifted his head. His scorching gaze slammed through her, making her clit throb, her pussy clench. A warm wetness dampened her inner thighs. Her panties were soaked. "You're in charge here, Bella," he said, his voice breaking on the words. "You make the rules."

"And no fucking whips and chains." He chuckled. Incensed by his mocking tone, she fisted his hair and yanked. "And no goddamn nipple clamps."

"Yes, ma'am."

As though she'd reminded him she had nipples, he thumbed them, then brought his fingers together. Tightly. The pinch made her knees go weak. She hissed, a sound somewhere between a sigh and a feral groan.

"You like that? You like it a little rough?" His voice was silky and smooth. Practiced. As though he'd said these words before. To thousands of women.

"Fuck you, Holt." She glared at him. When he grinned, laughed at her vehemence, she wrenched him closer. This time she took his mouth. Ravaged his mouth. Fucked his mouth. She thrust in her tongue, explored, dominated him.

Yeah. He'd fucked legions. But he would remember her. He would fucking remember her.

She'd make damn sure of it.

CHAPTER FOUR

Holy God.

He'd always suspected. He'd always known Bella would be a tigress in bed. But he hadn't realized. Hadn't really known just how wild she could be.

It inflamed him.

All rational thoughts evaporated. Thoughts of a sweet seduction, thoughts of gentle coaxing, thoughts of tender temptation.

Holt was possessed by one singular need.

Sinking into her.

He'd wanted her for so long. Fantasized about her. Obsessed over her. It had killed him that every time he'd so much as glanced at her, she'd scowled back at him. Her nose had wrinkled. Lips pursed.

He'd been convinced she hated him. Hated his lifestyle at least.

Now he wasn't so sure.

He'd always been good at reading women. He could sniff out a sub in a crowded room. He'd never gotten that vibe from Bella. But when he'd pinched her nipples, he'd seen it. That look in her eyes. Just a flash, hooded and guarded, but he'd seen it.

As though she kept it buried so deeply, even she didn't know.

The knowledge set him on fire.

He ached to discover more. To learn all her hidden secrets.

But he knew better.

With Bella, he would have to allow her to reveal them. One at a time. When she was ready. This, he knew instinctively. It took everything in him to hold back, let her take the lead.

What he really wanted to do was yank off her damn jeans, and those pink panties he had spotted when he'd toyed with her clit earlier. What he really wanted to do was fuck her, hard and fast, right here, right now, against this wall.

Hell, what he really wanted was her draped over his knee, writhing, her creamy ass high and turning red with his handprints. He knew, deep in his heart, she'd like it. She'd love it. But he also knew they weren't there yet. By far.

He wanted those things, but he wanted something else more.

He wanted this to work between them.

He wanted something real with her.

So he willed the beast within to be patient. He let her take the lead. He let her flail him with her fury.

The feel of her nails scoring his skin, her soft tongue thrusting into his mouth, her heated crotch rubbing against his, made his pulse pound.

He wanted, needed, more.

Now.

"Bella." He broke away, though it nearly killed him. Her lids were hooded, her lips parted. Her breathing uneven. "We should move into the bedroom."

He should have just done it. Just picked her up—she was a tiny thing—and hauled her off to the room off the hall. The bed was big. And it had four posters—

Brutally, he squashed that thought.

They weren't there yet either.

It took some effort to remind himself. *She* needed to take the lead. And he needed to let her.

She blinked, as though it took a moment for his suggestion to filter through the lust. Then she slowly released him and nodded. "Okay."

God, it was hard letting her go. Releasing his hold on her exquisite curvy form. Easing away from her warmth, her softness.

But he was following her lead. Like a well-trained pup.

Into the bedroom.

That, in itself, was something pretty damn phenomenal.

Lane's room was the only bedroom on the first floor, but Lane wasn't coming this weekend. Holt loved that she headed for that room and not one of the others. Because it was closer.

Clearly, she was as anxious as he to get naked and naughty.

But once they were both in the room, she staring at him and he staring right back, an awkward silence descended. He could see the second thoughts swelling in her eyes.

Oh, hell no.

"What do you want me to do?" he asked. Again, pure instinct. Reading her. Hoping he got it right.

A question flickered across her brow.

"You're in charge, Bella. Remember?"

It was amazing, watching her expression change. From a welling resistance, to that hint of confusion, to realization. To determination. That made a pulse slam in his aching cock.

She licked her lips. "Strip."

Oh yeah.

Even though he was a man of experience, that one word made him feel like a virgin with his first woman.

He wanted to whip off his clothes, but knew better. He knew Bella. She was a bundle of contradictions. It stood to reason she would appreciate another recalcitrant soul.

So he did it slowly.

First he sloughed off his leather jacket, meticulously draping it over the back of the chair. Then he leisurely unbuckled his leather chaps, letting them fall to the floor.

He glanced at her just in time to see her swallow. She tracked his every move. Slowly, deliberately, he raised the hem of his black t-shirt, studying her face.

God, he loved her face. She was beautiful on a bad day with alabaster skin and wide baby blue eyes. Her delicate chin had a tiny cleft. He loved the wink of the diamond stud in her freckled nose. But right now, staring at his body like that, as he slowly revealed his abs and chest, with her lips parted and lust for him etched on every feature—she'd never been more desirable.

He paused with his shirt halfway off and her focus flicked upward. He smiled. She frowned.

"Do it," she whispered. Her fingers curled into fists, as though she had to restrain herself from finishing it for him.

He pulled his shirt all the way off and dropped it.

And waited.

"The pants too." Her voice cracked.

He pulled out his wallet first. Opened it and found the foil packet. Tossed it on the bed. She watched his movements like a starving woman. Then he fiddled with his belt buckle. He took his time, because he was enjoying this too damn much to rush.

She fidgeted, shifting from one foot to the other. He sat on the chair and removed his boots. Then stood and unsnapped his jeans. Her tongue snaked out to wet her lips. With excruciating slowness, he drew his zipper down.

"Do it."

Holding her gaze, he peeled the denim from his body.

Her attention skated downward, slowly, then stalled. Her features tightened as she fixated on his cock, still encased in his cotton briefs. He hooked his thumbs in the elastic and sloughed those off as well.

His cock, rampant and roused, sprang free.

Her lips parted, trembled. She breathed a sigh.

"Now what?"

She jumped a little, as though he had interrupted a reverie. But it didn't take her long to issue her next command.

"Undress me."

Holy God. If he hadn't been hard and aching before, he was now. Just hearing those words, from her, sent a scalding lust skittering along every screaming nerve. "Yes ma'am."

It wasn't a large room, but it seemed to take an eternity to cross it. He halted before her and looked down at her, reveling in the moment. Then he grasped the hem of her t-shirt and lifted it. The air gushed out of his lungs as he revealed her torso, and her bra-clad breasts. She lifted her arms and he slipped the shirt off.

Glorious. She was glorious.

She was a tiny thing, but perfectly shaped. His palm itched to cup her, but he didn't.

To hell with whips and chains. This was real discipline. And it was killing him.

But he was determined.

He knelt before her and unsnapped her jeans, easing them over her hips. To save time—because, frankly, his patience was wearing thin—he drew down her panties with them.

His breath caught as her smooth slit hove into view.

Mother of God.

She stepped out of her jeans and he whipped them out of the way. And he stared at her.

"Now what?" he croaked.

Words. Not flowing.

Thoughts, frozen.

Her scent, her heat, rose to greet him.

He ached for a taste.

When she didn't answer, other than to spread her legs infinitesimally, he did what he wanted. What he needed. What he ached for.

Without her permission, he set his hands on her hips and drew his tongue along her slit. Just traced it. Just a tease. For both of them.

She whimpered. Threaded her fingers in his hair. Tugged him closer.

Yeah. Okay. Permission enough.

He delved deeper, licking his way between her folds, seeking and discovering that hard nubbin sheathed within. He dabbed it. Circled it. Tested it with his tongue.

"Ah," she groaned and spread her thighs more.

He nuzzled in, glorying in her taste, her scent. It soaked into him, infused him, maddened him.

But he remained tentative. Cautious.

This was a seduction, still. Even though she was nearly bare assed naked. But it was killing him. He wanted to toss her onto the bed, cover her, sink inside.

She was wet. Ready. At least physically. He needed her ready on all levels. He needed her crazy for him. Aching for him. Wild for him.

"More," she growled, and his pulse leapt.

Yes. Yes. More.

He drew her clit between his lips and sucked, then fluttered his tongue over the swollen flesh. She gasped, groaned, arched into him.

He held her still, sinking his fingers into the sumptuous globes of her ass, and doubled his efforts. She was so lush. He loved the way her muscles clenched, the way her skin rippled to his touch.

She tasted like heaven. Ambrosia. A hot, wet woman, tremendously aroused.

When she broke away from him he winced. He didn't like that at all. But she broke away and headed for the bed. *That* he liked that very much.

He really liked that she dragged him with her. By the hair.

They settled down on the soft mattress, side by side. Chest to chest. He tugged a bra strap down, and then the other, slowly revealing the mounds of her breasts.

His breath stalled. He couldn't resist. He took one crest, and then the other, into his mouth, nuzzling, sucking, lapping. He pressed her breasts together, as he'd ached to do earlier, buried his face between them and breathed deep.

So soft. So sweet. So incredibly tantalizing.

She pulled his head up and kissed him, a gentle buss. He ached to take it to another level, to open his mouth and take her in. Guide her. Instruct her. Dominate her. The effort to hold back made him tremble.

Her palm skated over his chest, exploring. It was the first time she'd touched him like this. Really *touched* him. The tentative caress sent ripples of excitement down his spine. They nested at the base of his cock.

Fuck.

He wanted her.

He wanted her bad.

Lifting his head, he looked at her. Lust sizzled between them. He swallowed against the aching lump in his throat.

"Now what?" The question took every ounce of his flagging restraint.

Please God. Let her say "fuck me." Let her say "Fuck me, now."

CHAPTER FIVE

He was driving her crazy. Frustration screamed through her. This was Holt Lamm, for god's sake. Why was he being so tentative? She wanted him to fuck her. To lay her back, yank her thighs apart and shove that big, hard cock in deep.

But he didn't.

He kept saying "Now what?" in that tender, patient tone—

Her heart stuttered then thudded painfully.

Oh. God.

That was it.

He'd told her she was in charge. She made the rules. He was letting her take charge. He wouldn't do anything unless she told him to.

The idiot.

She should punish him. She should just command him to lick her pussy again until she came and then just thank him politely and walk away. But the smoldering cauldron in her womb wouldn't allow it. She needed him in her, deep and hard. And she needed it now.

"Where's that condom?"

The relief on his face was so profound, she felt a ping of guilt for making him wait, but she pressed it away. When it came to Holt, there was no need for guilt or pity or politesse.

Holt was a fortress. A fucking machine. There were no tender sentiments lingering in his soul of souls. She didn't have to worry about hurting his feelings or wounding his ego. He fucked women and walked away every day. She was no different. She was nothing to him.

Still, she liked the way he scrambled for that foil packet. She liked it a lot. He ripped it open and unrolled it over his cock. She watched, avidly tracking every move.

God, he was beautiful.

His cock was large, hard, insistent. She loved the fat head, the long, shaft, thickly veined, the nest of dark hairs at the base. His attention, as he pulled the latex in place, was absolute. Her gaze drifted over his face, his high cheekbones and the sharp chin covered with manly scruff.

He turned back to her, eyes alight, ready to say, "Now what?" once more and she couldn't help it. She cupped his cheeks and pulled him close and kissed him.

His breath gusted into her mouth; she'd surprised him with her greedy attack, but he settled into it. Settled into her. He pressed her back on the bed and nudged her thighs apart. Her bra, still wrapped around her torso, bothered her, but his chest, scraping against her bare nipples, distracted her from that discomfort.

And then—dear God—something else distracted her. Distracted her entirely.

He found her entrance, slick and ready, and slipped in.

She groaned as he filled her. Shivers of delight racked her. God. It was amazing. He was amazing.

He huffed out a breath as he seated himself inside her. Shuddered. His cock pulsed, "N-now what?" She loved that his voice cracked when then said those damn words.

"Fuck me, Holt. Fuck me hard."

Something flared in his eyes. He lifted his hips and pushed her legs farther apart, opening her. But the move tightened her as well. She bit back a whimper.

She was not a whimperer. She would not whimper.

He pulled out and thrust in again, and again. Each lunge in a new direction. Finding, stroking, delighting a new bundle of weeping nerves with each foray. She couldn't help it. She grabbed his ass, clutching him, guiding him.

But he needed no guidance. Somehow, he knew just what to do. Just how to move.

Tension rose within her as he worked away, breathing into her ear in little puffs. She groaned as he hit a particular spot. He stilled for a second and then deliberately did it again.

"Yes," she huffed. "Yes. There."

He growled something in his throat and changed angles, increasing his pace, pummeling her with a manic barrage. He sucked a nipple into his mouth. Nibbled. Bit.

The sharp pain surprised her, but what surprised her even more was the wash of arousal it evoked. "God, yes," she snarled, planting her feet on the bed and arching up into him.

"You like that?" He didn't wait for a response. Did it again.

Waves of delight and agony and need raced through her. The

juxtaposition of sensation, the stinging at her breast, the singing of her womb, all befuddled her. Her brain ceased to function. She was nothing, nothing but a welter of pleasure. A desperate woman, filled to the brim with the cock of the man she wanted more than anything. The man she had wanted forever.

It was fucking awesome.

He yanked out and she winced, clung to him, but he pulled away. She was about to wail, protest, complain, when he flipped her over.

One strong hand to her hip. A flick of his wrist. As though she were thistledown, he turned her. Lifted her hips. Yanked her legs apart.

And, before she could process this new position, he drove in. Deep.

Everything in her seized.

God. Fuck. Shit.

This new position, with him looming over her, grasping the cheeks of her ass, guiding her movements, controlling her, plowing in and in, made her weak. Telltale shivers skittered through her lower body. Little flutters, harkening her impending explosion, grew. She sucked in a lungful of air and pushed back against him as he fucked her, fighting for domination. When that didn't work, she tightened around him. He stilled, buried deep inside, and shuddered, groaned. So she did it again.

His response was feral, a growl that might have been her name.

He took her hips in a tight grasp and held her steady, though she wanted to move. Wanted him to resume that manic pile-driving action that had her so close to rapture. But he didn't.

Slowly, he pushed her away. She shuddered as he withdrew. Then he eased her back, impaling her. Again and again. Tormenting her with his agonizing patience.

With each long slow drag, he filled her. Perfectly.

Also, as she moved back and forth beneath his guiding hand, her nipples scraped over the bedspread, sending shards of exquisite pain through her.

She ached. Everywhere. Twitched with impatience and need. So close to coming. So close…

The palm, landing on her ass, shocked her.

The sharp sting, certainly. But the shot of pure, unadulterated scalding lust shocked her even more.

She whipped her head around and stared at him over her shoulder. His features were tight. His jaw clamped. His nostrils flared. He drew his palm over the burning spot on her ass. "Now what, Bella?" He paired the question with a tiny thrust, as though he wanted to hold back, torment her, but he just couldn't hold back completely.

It nearly undid her.

That tiny little thrust.

It told her, showed her, he was as crazed as she.

No matter what. No matter what happened tomorrow or the day after that or the day after that, he wanted her now.

"Do it Holt. Fuck me hard."

The expression on his face made her quiver. Hot, hard, hungry man. A beast. A warrior. A dominant male.

His palm landed again and sensation scorched her. She wailed, but pushed back against him, clutching his cock with wet folds. He shivered. Pulsed inside her.

And then he went wild.

He still held her steady, but this time, he was the one moving. Hard. Fast. Deep. He pounded into her in a wild welter, a barrage of thrusts and lunges and manic plunges, each accompanied by a guttural groan.

"Yes," he growled. "Yes. Yes. Yes."

Her ass stung. Her nipples burned. Her womb ached.

That small flutter swelled.

Bella knew she was close. Knew that her crisis was upon her.

She arched up and looked back at him. Their gazes locked. She saw the panic, the desperation, the cataclysm in his eyes.

"Bella." He mouthed her name. And then, louder. "Bella."

His cock swelled. Surged.

He released his tight hold on her hips, hunched over her and slipped a hand between her legs, seeking and finding her hard, wet, clit.

It took one pass. One tender, tentative pass, and she came.

The ripples deep within grew as the wave spread outward. Swelling and welling and filling her soul. Pleasure swamped her. She closed her eyes and cradled her head in her arms.

And then, at the very peak—the peak she'd known many times before—his fingers closed. On her. On her clit. And he tugged.

Something. Something completely knew, utterly foreign in her experience, took her, ate her raw. This new sensation, an orgasm unlike anything she'd ever felt, consumed her, possessed her, whipped through her like a wildfire in a summer-dry forest.

He came with her, his jerking cock scraping over her super-sensitized flesh as he spasmed, driving her higher and higher still. Like a lost soul, she thrashed, wailed.

And then, as the storm settled, she melted beneath him onto the bed. When he slipped out and pulled her into his arms, a tiny whimper escaped her lips.

Never. Never before had she known such bliss.

She doubted she ever would again.

* * * * *

At some point, they fell asleep.

Bella had no idea how that happened, but when she opened her eyes again it was morning. They still lay crossways on the bed where they'd collapsed. Sometime in the night, Holt had covered them both with a blanket, and brought pillows around. He cradled her gently, spooning her back. His arm was a heavy weight on her hips.

He shifted, making her suspect he was awake and had been for a while, just waiting for her to rouse. She moved restlessly, though she hadn't intended to do so. Something long and hard and warm surged against her buttocks.

"Good morning." His voice rumbled through her, scratchy with sleep, or perhaps worn thin by his growls the night before.

She tried not to stiffen and failed. "Morning," she muttered.

Honestly. How could a man's morning breath be so tantalizing? It skated over her cheek as he bent to kiss her. She turned her head and the kiss landed on her ear. He nuzzled. Shivers of delight slid through her. Her body softened. Heat pooled in her belly.

He stroked her breast through the blanket. Even through that thick fabric, a bolt of electricity slammed her when he nudged her nipple.

Just nudged the fucker, for God's sake.

She'd always had the hots for Holt. Always. But that didn't mean she was easy.

He should at least have to try a little harder. Other men had to.

Hell, some men had to try for hours to get her to this point. All he had to do was fucking *breathe* on her.

If that wasn't confirmation of how dangerous this guy could be, she didn't know what was.

Last night, in the grip of lust—and whiskey—she'd imagined she could have him, take him, fuck him once. Yeah. Once. That would be enough. Then she could walk away knowing, finally knowing, what it was like.

This morning, her resolve was not so strong.

Not with him cradling her in his arms and stroking her nipple and nuzzling her ear. His damp mouth skimmed over her neck, leaving a warm trail that sent shivers through her as it cooled. His teeth scraped that one spot, just at her nape, the one that made her all achy and soft.

It annoyed her that he'd found it so easily when others had failed. Some of her lovers had never found that spot.

It was as though he knew exactly what to do to turn her on, and he did it. Unrepentantly.

She gasped as he whipped back the covers and turned her over. Sometime in the night he'd removed her bra. She was naked. He dipped his head and took a nipple into his mouth and, before she could so much as protest, sucked.

A whimper slipped out.

She tried to swallow it, but couldn't. It was far too insistent.

She should stop him. Really. She should. They weren't doing this again. Couldn't. Shouldn't...

He found her nest and he dandled her clit, rubbing it in a circular motion with just the right amount of pressure. Her thighs parted.

Maybe a moment. Just a moment more and then she'd stop him.

He slipped deeper, easing two fingers into her pussy. They slid right in. She could tell she was wet. Soaked. He groaned and the sound vibrated through the nipple in his mouth. He nibbled it. She clenched him in a tight grasp.

Something—possibly a tiny orgasm—walked through her.

It couldn't be an orgasm. Not even a tiny one. She wasn't easy. Not *that* easy, anyway.

But when he raised his head and locked gazes with her and shoved in another finger, working her, rubbing her, massaging her just where it counted, she realized she was wrong.

She was that easy.

She came in a flood. A flood of sensation.

It was one of the sweet ones. A lazy, effortless early-morning orgasm that rose up like a gentle tide and swamped her.

And all the while, as he led her, guided her, skillfully drew her along, he watched her, a scorching intensity simmering his chocolate brown eyes.

CHAPTER SIX

She came beautifully.

He'd wanted to see that. He'd had a glimpse last night, when she came on his lap, and again when she'd glanced at him over her shoulder as he'd been buried in her cunt. But this—this was different. Face to face. Almost nose to nose. He could see it all, playing over her delicate features. The confusion, the resistance and then, finally, the acceptance and release.

And she was glorious in her release.

Once she was done, once her body had ceased to tremble and he had soothed her, he drew back and brought his fingers to his lips. Tasted her.

He shuddered. Yes. This was her. Bella. Her essence.

His cock twitched. He needed her. Again.

Then again, he'd awakened needing her.

He levered up, preparing to cover her, to slip inside, but before he could, she leapt from the bed.

"Oh no," she said, raking her hair. It was wild and long and unkempt. He loved it. "We can't. We shouldn't have…"

His gut clenched. He'd suspected this. Expected it. Nothing with Bella was ever easy. But he'd be damned if he would make this easy for her.

He leaned on his elbow and watched her hunt for her clothes in a room strewn with clothes. "Shouldn't have what?"

She whirled on him with a frown. "Shouldn't have…" she waved a hand toward the bed. Toward him. *"That."*

"Fucked?"

"Yes! Fucked." She found her t-shirt and pulled it on. He hated seeing her breasts disappear, but they were still pretty damn splendid, cradled in cotton. "We shouldn't have fucked. I was…" He smiled because he knew what was coming. "I was drunk."

"Are you saying I took advantage of you?" Might as well go on the

29

offensive.

She froze. Her gaze flicked to him. Her lips parted. Damn. Those lips. He'd love to feel them wrapped around his cock right now.

He'd love to feel anything wrapped around his cock right now. It ached like the devil.

He threw back the covers and stood, noting with pleasure that her attention fixed on just that.

"Are you? Saying I took advantage of your inebriated state?"

She swallowed. Forced her attention to his face. "N-no."

Relief trickled through him. Although he knew it wasn't true, it mattered to hear her admit it.

"But we shouldn't have."

"Why not?"

She blew out an impatient breath and picked up a pair of jeans, shoving her legs in. He nibbled on his lower lip. They were his jeans.

They looked damn cute on her, but they were way too big.

She realized her mistake, kicked them off and growled something under her breath as she found her own. He waited until she had her armor on to repeat his question. "Why not?"

She glared at him. Her lips worked. "Because, Holt!"

"Not an answer. Why should we not have fucked, and might I add, rather magnificently, last night?"

Her lashes flickered. "Magnificently?" A small voice.

"*Rather* magnificently."

She threaded her fingers together and pursed her lips. "We don't even like each other, Holt."

He quirked a brow. "We covered this Bella. We like each other plenty." He waved at the bed. "Plenty enough."

"You're a Dom."

"We covered that too." He stepped closer, because her arguments were waning, her expression softening. "You took the lead last night. I did everything you asked. And that worked out pretty good."

She crossed her arms. Her breasts thrust out. He disciplined himself to focus on her face.

"I didn't ask you to smack my ass." She flushed as soon as she said it.

"No you did not." He paused, giving her a moment to think about it before he added softly, "Did you hate it?"

Her flush turned a rosy red. "I— That's not the point."

"It is exactly the point. If you hated it, if you told me never to do it again, I would not. On that you have my solemn vow. And that goes for everything, Bella. If you told me never to do this again," he cupped her breast and thumbed a nipple. "I would never do that again." He drew a slow circle. Her nipple swelled to a hard point. "Do you want to ask me not to do that again?"

Her lips parted. Her eyes dewed. "I—"

"Or this?" He found and stroked that spot on her nape. As he knew she would, she shuddered. "Do you want to ask me not to do that again?"

"Holt—"

"Or this?" He kissed her. Slowly. Softly. A light drag of his lips over hers. Maybe a hint of tongue. She tipped up her chin and followed him when he retreated. "Just say the word, Bella. Just say the word and I will never do any of that again. But know this." He held her steady, so she couldn't look away. "I want you. I've wanted you for years. I want you like I've never wanted another woman."

Her lips parted as though she would refute this claim. He did not give her the chance.

"I would do anything for a chance to be with you. In whatever way you see fit. Do you understand?"

She swallowed. Nodded.

"Do you feel the same? Would you like to explore…whatever this is? With me?"

He waited, on bated breath, for her answer.

He hoped she said yes.

Bella stared at Holt, her pulse thudding a manic tattoo.

She got it. She totally got it. She totally understood why a woman would curl up at his feet and give him anything. Offer him everything.

A part of her rebelled at the concept of being a slave to any man, but a greater part of her, a hungrier part of her, craved it. It whipped through her like a howling wind.

Hunger. No, more than that. Yearning for this man.

Did she want to explore this insanity, this burning, roiling, festering ache—an ache she'd carried with her for far too long? Yes. Hell yes.

But the word caught in her throat. So she merely nodded.

Heat skirled through his eyes. A little of the tension eased from his expression. But his lips firmed. "Say it, Bella. I need to hear it."

"Yes, Holt."

Before she'd finished, before the last consonant of his name escaped, he yanked her into his arms, hard against him. His mouth covered hers and he consumed her with a needy kiss.

When he raised his head, they were both breathless. Lust sizzled through her veins. Her nipples were taut, her pussy dripping. Why she had bothered to get dressed was a mystery.

He pressed a quick buss on her forehead. Then a longer one, murmuring something to himself as he made his way along her hairline. It sounded like, "Excellent."

She thought he was going to strip her then, whip off her shirt and toss her onto the bed. He looked like he wanted to. His cock certainly looked like he wanted to. But he didn't. He stepped back and tucked a lock of her hair behind her ear.

"Let's have some breakfast," he said.

She gaped. "B-breakfast?"

He grinned. "Trust me, Bella. We're going to need our strength."

He made pancakes from the gluten-free mix in the pantry and fried up bacon while she cleaned up the mess on the patio. The whiskey bottle had leaked all over the deck and her cigarettes were a soggy mess so she got a trash bag and threw it all away. Then she made the coffee while he finished up the food. They didn't speak, but for once, the energy between them wasn't awkward in the slightest.

Bella found herself stealing glances at him while he cooked, but who could blame her? While he'd pulled on his jeans, he hadn't bothered with a shirt. And with every move he made, his biceps rippled beneath velvety nut-brown skin.

She loved that he was so tall and muscular. He made her feel like a petite doll. She rarely felt petite.

Normally she would never eat a whole pancake, but his were so good, she had two. And the bacon was to die for. She ate all her slices and then, to his gentle ribbing, stole some of his.

She'd worry about her diet tomorrow.

When he finished eating, he slid his plate away, cupped his mug and looked at her across the table. Though they sat apart, that broad width between them, their feet had tangled throughout the meal. Bare feet tangling, she decided, was very sexy.

"So we should talk," he said.

"Okay." She took one more bite of pancake and set down her fork. "About what?"

He tipped his head to the side and traced the lip of his cup. "Limits."

"L-limits?"

"I think it's important. Don't you?"

She gulped. "I suppose."

"Let's start with the basics."

"O-okay." Hell. She'd never had a sex negotiation before.

"For example, I don't do men."

"I do." It was supposed to be a joke, to lighten her tension, maybe, but he didn't laugh.

He simply fixed her with a steady gaze and asked: "Do you do women?"

She choked on her breath. "I…ah…no."

"Multiple partners?"

"Definitely no."

"Good. Me either." He reached across the table and covered her hand with his. "When I'm with a woman, she is my only focus. My whole world." His voice cracked a little on the word.

"I…ah… Yeah. Me too."

"So what kinds of things won't you do?"

She shook her head. "I don't really know what we're talking about here, Holt."

He nodded. "Okay. When I smacked your ass. Did you like that?"

Heat scorched her. She turned away. His hold on her tightened. "Look at me please, Bella. It helps if I can see your expression." She complied. "Did you like when I smacked your ass?"

"Y-yes." A whisper.

"Okay. Good. That's probably something I'll do again."

"P-probably?" She burbled the word.

He grinned, revealing that he had, in fact, been teasing.

Oh, not about smacking her ass again. Sometime. In the near future. No. He hadn't been teasing about that.

"I'd really like to give you a paddling…" He shifted restlessly. But then, so did she. "I'd also like to tie you up, but before you said something about that. Have you ever been tied up, Bella?"

Jesus. He looked so sincere. Spoke those words in such a fucking normal tone. As though he had conversations like this over pancakes and bacon all the time.

The thought pissed her off.

She was so pissed off, she forgot to control her reaction to his question.

His eyes narrowed. "You have. Haven't you?"

"Yes." A mutter. It had been a dismal experiment with an even more dismal partner.

"You didn't like it?"

"No." She'd hated it. The loss of control, the creeping fear. The panic when he wouldn't untie her. She snorted and tried to make a joke of that miserable memory. "I had rope burns for a week."

He stilled. "Rope burns?" A low snarl. "Why would you have rope burns?"

She opened her mouth. Closed it again. God. She didn't want to relive this. Not with him.

"Why, Bella?"

"You know. From struggling to get free."

His voice, when he spoke, was a slithery snake. "Why would you need to struggle to get free?" Ooh. This Holt scared her a little. She scooted her chair back. Just a bit.

"He wouldn't…"

"He wouldn't untie you? Did you ask?"

God yes. Begged. Until her throat was raw. She nodded. Nibbled her lip.

"Fucker," he growled. Bella jumped when his palm slammed on the table. Her gaze snapped to Holt's face. She winced at what she saw there. Rage.

She cowered a little when he stood in a rush and came around the table. He was so big. So strong. And she felt so vulnerable right now. But he hunkered down at her feet and took her hand and kissed it gently. Reverently.

"I will never, ever, ever, never, ever do that to you. Do you understand?"

"Umm hmm." She was speechless. Because all that fury, all that rage, was on her behalf. No one had ever smacked a table for her before.

"If we ever do that, it will only be because you want to and you expressly ask for it. And by all that is holy, the moment you say 'untie me, Holt' you are fucking free. Do you understand?"

"Umm hmm."

He looked up at her and tried to smile, but she could still see anger simmering behind his eyes. He sat in the seat next to her, but didn't let go of her. "I mean it, Bella. It's a partnership. We're in this together. Anytime you want me to stop what I am doing, no matter what it is… If I'm fucking you and a breath away from coming and you don't like something, you say your safe word and that's it. It stops."

"My…safe word?"

He blinked. "You do know what a safe word is?"

She blew out a breath. "I read. Of course I know what a safe word is. I just…well, I don't have one. Hell, I don't even know how to pick one."

"It's easy." He stroked her palm with his thumb. "Some people go with 'red light', because red means stop. Some people pick a word they might normally use, but would never say during sex. Like…bacon." He shot her a playful grin.

"No." She tapped her lips. "I might say that during sex."

His chuckle warmed the room. "Okay then. What would you never say during sex?"

She snorted.

"What?"

"Oh, it's…God. The one word I would never ever say during sex?"

"Yeah?"

"Kristi."

He gaped at her, then threw back his head and laughed. "Yeah, that would kill the mood I guess."

She frowned at him. She'd forgotten. He had a thing for her sister. "It would kill the mood for me. Might spur you on." She didn't mean to say it quite like that, with so much bitterness. But she did.

He noticed. His lips tightened. "It would not spur me on."

"Tell me you don't have a crush on her."

"I don't."

"Everyone has a crush on her."

"I don't."

"I saw the way you looked at her the last time we were all here. I saw—"

"I fucking don't. Get this through your thick, stubborn head, Bella. I've never had a thing for Kristi. Not the way I—" He broke off. A red tide rose on his cheeks.

He would have leapt to his feet, escaped perhaps, but she held tight to his hand. "Not the way you what?"

He blew out a breath. Scrubbed his face with a palm. "We've covered this Bella." He met her wary gaze. "You're the one I want."

"Right now. You know. 'Cause I'm here and all."

"You're the one I want."

Something, maybe the waver in his tone, convinced her. At least for now. She was the one he wanted. For now. She would take what she could get.

"Okay then. Kristi it is."

He blinked. "What?"

Her lips curved in a sly smile. "My safe word. Is Kristi. And if it spurs you on, I'll kill you."

CHAPTER SEVEN

Once their negotiations were finished, Holt suggested, with the waggle of his brow, that they hop into the hot tub before they began. Since Bella wanted to take a quick shower first, she asked him to dig her bathing suit out of her suitcase, which she shouldn't have done.

Because she'd forgotten.

She'd stopped by the supplier on the way to the island and the samples were tucked in her bag.

Yeah.

Dildos and floggers and the dreaded nipple clamps.

She stepped out of the bathroom to find him sitting on the living room floor with toys strewn all around him like a kid at Christmas.

"Oh, hell." Heat crawled up her cheeks as she watched him finger a leather collar with metal studs. "Give me that." She snatched it from him. She did not understand the glint in his eye. "What?" she snapped.

"You know, when a sub takes a collar from her Master, it has a special meaning."

She tried to glower, but his grin was too engaging. "I am not taking a collar from you—"

"Yeah, I think you just did—" He winked.

"And you are not my Master." Yet.

He arched a brow. They had agreed to one trial session. With her as the meek little sub. She didn't hold out hope she could make it through without bursting into manic laughter. Or punching him in the gut.

He'd offered to take it slow, but she'd dredged up her courage and told him not to hold back. If she was going to try this, she should try it all the way. Shouldn't she?

Only now she wasn't so sure...

He held up a package. "This looks interesting."

"What is it?" She leaned closer. She hadn't paid any attention to the new items her distributor had foisted upon her. She was planning to go through all that stuff on Monday.

"An egg."

"An egg?"

He waggled his brow. "With variable controls. And a remote."

Ooh. She didn't like his expression.

Or maybe she did.

"And this…" He picked up a leather flogger with knots tied along the multiple tails. He glanced at her. "Probably too much to start with."

She gulped. "St-start with?"

"This one is better." A slender wand with a flap on the end. The flap had a little heart cutout.

"Cute."

His expression was wicked. "Maybe we should put off the hot tub until later. What do you say to a game of 8-Ball?"

This change of topic surprised her. She blinked at him. "You want to play pool?"

"Did I say pool, little slave?"

"I'm not your slave."

"I think I said 8-Ball."

"I'm not your slave."

He ignored her, making a pile of items and tossing the rest back into her suitcase, which he zipped closed. She was delighted beyond words to see the collar and the leather restraints go back in the bag. He did, however, leave an evil-looking halter out. And the egg. And the flogger. He came to his feet and took her hand. "What do you say? Are you game for…a game?"

She pursed her lips. Oh, sure. It had been one thing talking about this over the dining room table. It was another thing entirely now. Three feet away from that table. "No."

He tipped his head to the side and studied her. "No is not your safe word. No doesn't stop anything. You understand that?"

She swallowed the lump in her throat. Nodded.

"So if I don't hear that very special word…I'm going to assume you're just being a brat—"

"I'm not a brat."

"A *brat* who wants more punishment."

God, he was so sexy, standing there like that, staring at her. Like that. The sensuality simmering in his eyes. The scratchy scruff on his chin. Those full lips…

Excitement lashed her.

She was good at being a brat. She kind of liked that he was encouraging it.

And the thought of punishment... Why did that make her nipples tighten? Dampness pool between her thighs?

Oh, she knew why.

What really turned her on was the fact that he knew too.

"So we're agreed? We both understand the rule?"

"The r-rule?"

"No safe word, no stopping?"

Something caught in her throat. She swallowed heavily. Nodded.

"I need to hear you say it, Bella."

"Yes, Holt. Only my safe word really means no."

He squeezed her fingers. "Okay. Let's go downstairs."

"Down-downstairs?"

"Umm hmm. Pool table's downstairs."

"You said you didn't want to play pool."

He narrowed his gaze on her. "Are you talking back?"

The way he said it. That harsh tone... It sent a sizzle through her womb. "N-no."

"Call me Sir, if you please, Bella."

"S-sir?" Why was she stuttering?

"Indulge me." He waited, studying her as she worked up the courage.

It took a while.

"S-sir." A whisper.

Only a whisper, but the change in him was dramatic. His expression went firm and stern. His beautiful lips pulled down into a frown. "Well, darling? What are you waiting for?" She turned to head for the basement, but he stopped her. "Aren't you forgetting something?"

"Hmm?"

He waved at the toys on the floor. She gulped. "You want me to carry them?"

His grin was wolfish.

The basement, the rec room, took on a new light somehow as Bella made her way down the stairs carrying the implements of her impending torture. For some reason, the thought of that impending torture didn't scare her in the least. It should. But it didn't. She trusted Holt to keep his word and stop if she said the magic word.

Still, her pulse fluttered as she stepped off the last stair into the darkened room. It could have been a dungeon. There were sofas and chairs strewn around the large screen television, but a large pool table dominated the room. Balls were neatly racked at one end.

"Go ahead. Put those things on the table," he said. And then he stood and watched as she did just that, diligently arranging each item next to the racked balls. She hated that she trembled. "Nice. Good girl."

He seemed taller in the shadows. More menacing, perhaps. Definitely hotter than he'd ever looked before. It was probably the scorching hunger in his eyes.

"And now, if you will, please remove your clothing."

Her pulse leapt. "W-what?"

"There's something you should know Bella. I require immediate compliance to all my commands. Hesitation will only earn you a punishment."

She opened her mouth to respond. To issue some scathing retort, but then snapped it shut. Most likely, snark would earn her a punishment as well.

And she had agreed to this trial. To see if she liked this. Only to see if she liked this.

She might as well play by his rules.

She liked that she had a choice. She could say the word now and go back upstairs and he would probably never mention this little experiment again.

But she didn't want to.

She really didn't want to.

She'd fantasized about something like this all her adult life. Fantasized about him. But those fantasies had been locked in her imagination. Locked in the scorching pages on her e-reader where every hero, every Dom, had Holt's face.

It scared her to death, taking this step. But she needed to do it.

Slowly she removed her t-shirt and dropped it on the floor.

"Fold it, please."

His face was tight, hungry, but she sensed in him phenomenal restraint. She bent and retrieved her shirt and folded it neatly.

It was a novel experience for her.

She never folded anything.

"And your jeans."

She kicked them off and folded them as well, setting her clothes on a pile on the back of the sofa. She hadn't bothered to put on her underwear earlier, so she was naked.

There wasn't a breeze, but she felt the ambient air stir against her bare skin. She shivered as goose bumps rose.

He stepped closer. Drifted his fingers over her shoulder, her collarbone, down to her breast. Why this made her tremble, she had no clue. "You are so beautiful Bella. So beautiful."

He turned to the pool table and selected one of the items she'd set out. She winced when she got a peek. The halter.

"Do you know what this is?"

Not really. She shook her head.

"Here, then. Let me help you put it on." He eased the halter around her torso and fit it in place over her breasts. She was preternaturally aware of the scrape of his knuckles as he worked. When he finished adjusting straps and buckling her in, she realized it was a leather bra-like contraption with adjustable cups. He held her gaze and tightened a strap. And another.

She sucked in a breath as her breasts squeezed into concentric circles, each tighter than the last, until the final ring, around her aureoles where they formed tight points. He thumbed a nipple, then pinched. She winced.

"Are you okay?" A soft murmur. A soothing rumble.

"Yes."

"Yes *Sir*."

"Y-yes Sir." She swallowed. Looked down.

He tipped her chin back up. "I like to see your expression, Bella." He went back to the table and came back with more straps and she realized, the bra portion was only the half of it. There was also a belt that fit around her waist and around the top of her thighs. She couldn't imagine what the purpose of it was, but she didn't ask.

He stepped back to survey his work. "Nice." He turned her toward the mirror and she gasped.

Holy hell. Just that much. Just a few straps and buckles here and there, and she looked like an honest to goodness submissive.

"See these rings here?" He touched the metal rings along the girdle. "If I was going to restrain your hands, I would fasten them here." He touched more rings on the halter. "Or here. But I'm not going to restrain your hands."

"Y-you're not?"

"No. You asked me not to." He paused. His intent flared between them. "But you are going to restrain your hands."

She spun on him, her mouth agape. "What?"

His smile was sinful. "You'll see. Now then…" He rummaged through the items and came up with the egg. "This, I think."

"That?" she squeaked.

He ripped open the package without answering and pulled out the oblong vibrator. Deftly, he opened it and fit the batteries in place. When he snapped it shut, the click echoed through the room.

"Lay on the table, Bella. Here." He patted the felt.

She shot him a wary glance, but did not hesitate, she knew better than that, levering up onto the table at one end and lying down. The baize was soft and rough at the same time, teasing her bare skin.

He readjusted her, pulling her further toward the end, so her ass rested on the lip of the table, her hips at a slight slant.

"Open your thighs."

She closed her eyes and did as he asked. Winced when something cold touched her clit. "Open your eyes Bella."

She did. The egg turned on and a ripple of vibration shot through her. She shot up.

He didn't need to say anything. His look said it all. Slowly, she laid back down and spread her legs again. This time when he touched her, she didn't move. She held her muscles tight and willed her body to stay as still as she could.

He played with her clit for a while, running the smooth head of the egg around and around and then, finally, he slipped it inside. The buzzing became muted. Although she felt every frenetic vibration to her core.

His grunt echoed in the silence. "You're wet."

"Y-yes Sir."

Warmth suffused her at the gratitude she saw in his eyes.

"Put your arms over your head."

She did so, slowly, reveling in the caress of the rough fabric on her back as she moved.

He rounded the table, his fingers trailing up her thigh, over her mound, along her torso and over her breasts as he passed. "Are you ready to play 8-Ball?"

She shot him a grin. "I thought we were already playing."

The sharp sting at her breast surprised her. She hadn't noticed him pick up the little crop with the flap. But she felt it. Her whole body lurched. Her pussy clenched on the vibrator and heightened the sensations. Electricity singed through her. She shuddered.

"Are you talking back?" His voice was harsh.

"N-no sir."

He paused. Dipped his head and kissed the redness on her breast. "Are you okay?" he murmured, gauging.

He was close, so she didn't need to say it loudly. "Yes...Sir." On a breath.

His tongue shot out and dabbed at his lips. He stared at her, as if poleaxed, then abruptly stood. "Okay. Let's begin. Open your palms."

He arranged her, palms up, and set something heavy and hard in them. It took her a moment to realize he'd set two pool balls in each palm. "Hold on to these. If you drop them, there will be a punishment. Do you understand?"

"Yes Sir."

"This is what I meant when I said you will be restraining your own hands."

Holy crap, he was devious. But she could do this.

However, he wasn't done yet. He grabbed the cue ball and made his way back to the end of the table.

"Close your legs." She brought her knees together until they met an obstruction. Another ball. She clenched it between her legs. "Hold that there. Do not drop it. If you drop it, there will be a punishment. Do you understand?"

"Y-yes Sir."

Okay, that one took some focus.

"And one more ball." He held it up for her to see. The 8-Ball. This one he settled on her belly. It wobbled with every breath and because her hips were at an angle, it listed toward her ribs. "Hold it there. Don't let it fall. If it falls—"

"I know. I know. If it falls, there will be a punishment."

Okay. She should have bit her tongue and just let him finish his stupid little statement, but she was too busy focusing on the stupid balls to remember not to be snarky.

This time the little flap, the one with the heart-shaped cut out, landed right on her pussy. She flew up into the air and all the balls fell.

Holt surveyed her with a small pout on his face. Then he tsked. Goddamn it. She hated it when people tsked.

"Bella, Bella, Bella. What did I say?"

She tried, very hard, not to roll her eyes. "Punishment."

"Punishment." He tsked again and she wanted to strangle him but she couldn't. There was probably a punishment for that too.

He eased her back down on the table and arranged her into position. Patiently, he set the balls back in her hand, the cue ball between her knees and the 8-ball on her belly. He tapped his lips with the flap of that tiny crop, the one that didn't feel so small when it landed.

She didn't like the looks of that.

"One lash for each ball, Bella."

"Wh—" She squeezed her lips shut before the screech came all the way out and her restraint seemed to placate him.

"Are you ready?"

"Yes Sir." A grumble.

"Hold tight to your balls." She'd like to hold tight to his… "Okay, count with me, Bella."

"Ah!" The first lash fell. You'd think he'd warm up to it, start easy or something, but he didn't. It landed right on her throbbing nipple. She didn't lose any balls. But, all of a sudden, her pulse was very pronounced. In her clit. God help her if he decided to land one of those lashes there.

"Count with me, Bella."

"One." Through gritted teeth.

The second lash fell on her other nipple. "Two."

He paused and she tensed, imagining where he would strike next. Please

God. Please not there…

No.

On the same nipple, the right nipple, which still stung like hell. "Th-three."

The same nipple again! God damn him, it hurt! "Four."

She took a breath, checked her balls. Thankfully, they were all still in place, though the one between her knees was slipping a little and the 8-ball on her belly wobbled like mad.

The lash fell again—on her left nipple. Even though it sent shards of pain and warmth through her, she blew out a breath of relief. She didn't think she could take it if—

Without warning, the little flap fell again. And directly over her throbbing clit. She hadn't been expecting it. She hadn't been ready. Her legs jerked and while she kept hold of the balls in her hands, the one between her knees slipped free and thudded to the floor. The 8-ball rolled off her belly onto the table as well.

"Shit."

"You're really not very good at this game, are you Bella?" Amusement laced his tone.

She levered up on her elbow, careful not to drop her balls. "No fair. That was six, not five."

"Really?" Did I hear you count to five?"

She froze as his words sank in. Shit. She hadn't. She opened her mouth to make a pithy response. He didn't allow it.

"Besides, Bella. There's no such thing as fair in a game like this. You need to understand that. I'm the Master, and if I think you need another lash, you get another lash. Do you understand?"

She glared at him mutinously.

His benign smile annoyed her tremendously.

"And now, let's see. You dropped two balls. Two lashes per ball."

"Two?" She really should learn to shut up.

He fixed her with a dark look. "Shall we make it three?"

"N-no Sir." With a sigh she flopped back into position.

CHAPTER EIGHT

She survived the four lashes, remembering to count out each one, and she didn't drop a single ball. She remained tense when he had finished.

Her nipples were a little sore and her clit pulsed like the dickens. Still, she was very proud of herself. It was almost a disappointment that he didn't praise her.

But that was stupid.

Wasn't it?

When he finished, he turned away. She could hear him rummaging with items over by the cue stand but she didn't dare lift her head to peek, too afraid she would dislodge the ball on her belly.

When he came back, he held something behind his back. "Close your eyes, Bella," he said.

She did as he asked. And then she waited. Holding her breath. What would he do now?

The sensation, when she felt it, almost made her leap out of her skin. A rough scrape over one nipple, and then the other.

Oh. God. He had the baize brush.

A whimper escaped.

"Hold still." A murmur.

She held her breath as he tormented her with that brush, scraping it over one swollen nipple and then the other. She didn't wrench away, but it took everything in her to hold still. Her clench on the egg, thrumming away deep inside her, tightened though. It nearly made her crazy.

Oddly enough, the abrasion of the brush didn't hurt. Not really. But it sent a scalding heat along every nerve. Though when he skated it down and around her breasts, it tickled. She nearly wrenched away then. Even when he traced her tender underarms, up to her elbow and down again, she was able to maintain control, but it cost her.

It wasn't until he teased the brush down her leg, to the bottom of her foot, that she had her next accident. It was a knee jerk reaction. Literally. When those soft bristles danced over her arch, she just couldn't stop herself.

The cue ball, between her knees hit the floor.

He stopped immediately and picked it up.

Tsked again.

She glowered at him, even though she was still supposed to have her eyes closed.

"Five lashes."

Yeah. That horrified her, but not as much as his next move. He spread her knees and stepped between her legs and slid his fingers through the folds of her labia, holding her open. "Here, I think."

She sucked in a breath. Let go a little mewl. But said nothing. She lifted her head and watched, stared, as he raised the little crop. The first one was gentle, almost tender. He looked up at her, waiting.

She licked her lips. "One." A croak.

The second was a little harder. It landed directly on her clit. She winced. The 8-ball wobbled. "T-two."

The third actually echoed around the room, in concert with her wail. "Three!"

The 8-ball fell with the forth. And she lost all the balls with the fifth.

That was a total of five balls.

He'd upped the ante with each drop.

Dear God. How many would it be this time?

He let her stew, massaging the sting from her aching clit.

"H-Holt?" Her voice was small. Way too small.

He stilled. Their gazes locked. "You've earned a pretty big punishment, Bella. Do you-do you want to continue?"

She swallowed. God, he was giving her an out. She could take it. She should…

"Yes Sir. I want to continue."

A muscle bunched in his cheek. His tongue peeped out. His lips trembled.

And then he regained himself. His persona. His role.

"All right then. I think it's time to get serious."

She nearly howled.

"Turn over."

He helped her stand—her knees were wobbly—and draped her over the edge of the table. Her breasts, still in the constricting harness, ached and the baize scraped her nipples as she positioned herself. Her mound brushed against the edge of the table.

He adjusted her. "Hips up a bit. There." Something cold touched her clit. Shit. The damn 8-ball. He set it between her body and the table. If she released any pressure on it at all, it would fall to the floor. And then what would he do?

"Got it?"

"Yes Sir."

"Hold it steady."

"Yes Sir."

He stepped to the other side of the table and stretched out her arms, again, placing balls in her hand. "Hold on tight."

"Yes Sir." Her voice cracked because she saw what he picked up while he was down there. The flogger.

Shit!

She tensed as he returned to the foot of the table. His palm skated over her ass. She shivered, trying not to move, but when she did, the 8-ball rolled against her clit.

Oh God.

"Are you ready?" She could tell from his tone, he usually didn't bother to ask. But he was going easy on her.

"Y-yes Sir."

The lash fell. The sting was excruciating. Also excruciating, the roll of the ball over her clit. She hissed in a breath.

"Count for me Bella."

"One."

The vibrator in her cunt, which had been keeping up a nice steady rhythm, slowly but surely driving her closer and closer to orgasm, suddenly stopped. Then started. Then stopped again.

Then it set up an agonizing uneven cadence. She nearly went out of her mind.

But there was no time to focus on that. Because the next lash fell.

"Bella?"

His voice was sharp, but from far, far away.

"Two."

And another.

"Three."

And another.

"Four."

How many? How many could she take? With each lash the heat grew. The tantalizing roll against her clit, the agonizing uneven throb in her dripping pussy—

And then, all of a sudden, she realized a new danger.

The cream in her cunt, her frantic clenches on that egg…it was starting to slip out.

God, no!

"Holt! Holt!"

"Say the word, Bella."

"No. It's not that. The egg. It's slipping out!"

"Don't drop it, Bella. If you drop it, you will earn another punishment."

She nearly snarled at him. God damn it. She couldn't hold it in. She couldn't…

The lash fell again and she forgot to count. He had to prompt her. "Five." And then, "Six!"

The pattern of vibrations deep inside changed again. And again. Her pulse pounded against that damn 8-ball. Lash after lash fell, heating her ass, urging her forward, scraping her nipples against the felt. It was too much… It was too much… She couldn't… She…

She came. Exploded. With a feral bellow, with the rumble of balls as they tumbled from her hands, with the dull thud of the egg as it hit the floor.

The 8-ball, however, she managed to save.

God was she incredible.

For a first-timer, she'd done so incredibly well. He suspected she might be a natural sub under that prickly exterior.

No. He knew it. And he'd known it for a while.

After she came, he soothed her, rubbing her red ass and stroking his fingers into her sopping cunt.

God, he wanted in here.

In a minute. He needed to give her a moment to recuperate.

When she was ready, he turned her over on the table and drew her swollen nipples into his mouth and sucked gently. "You were wonderful, Bella," he murmured. "Just wonderful."

"Was I?"

He thumbed the tears from her cheeks. "Yes. You did very well." He kissed her cheek. Her nose. Her lids. Peppered her with devotion as he continued to stroke her slit. She was so ready.

He was so ready.

So needy.

"Are you ready to continue?"

Her eyes widened. "C-continue?"

"I need you, Bella."

"Hmm." She murmured. "Am I still your slave?"

"If you want to be."

"Maybe a bit longer."

He chuckled. "I do have a powerful need." He nudged his erection against her thigh. She attacked the snap of his jeans with alacrity and then, when his cock sprang free, she licked her lips.

God help him.

But as much as he wanted a blow job from her at some point, this was not that point. What he wanted now, what he needed now, was to be in her.

He kissed her and eased her back on the table. She responded with a groan, but it was a groan of arousal. He eased himself between her legs and fisted his cock, pointing it in the direction it desperately wanted to go.

He nearly lost consciousness as he brushed her damp heat. His pulse pounded, his head ached, his body howled for release.

And then, just when he was about to plunge into heaven, she stiffened and pushed at him. "No Holt. Wait."

"Umm hmm." He thrust his hips, reveling in the tight grip of her creamy walls.

"Holt. Stop."

"That's it, baby. Yeah." He loved the way she wriggled against him.

"Holt! Kristi!"

He froze. Jerked back. Stared down at her in shock.

Seriously?

Right now?

Right. Fucking. Now?

He yanked out. He had to. Like a bandage, one quick rip was the only way. But God, it stung. His pulse pounded painfully in his temple. Acid churned in his gut.

"I...what... What did I do wrong?"

Her brow wrinkled. "Wrong?"

"Why did you say 'Kristi?'"

"Because dumbass," she hissed. "I just heard her voice. Cam and Kristi are upstairs."

And just then, the back door slammed.

It was nearly comical, the way they both leapt up and yanked their clothes on. Holt took all the "toys" and shoved them under a sofa cushion. Except one. He tucked the egg in his pocket. Yeah, it made him look like he had an enormous bulge on one side of his pants, but it kind of evened things out.

Bella yanked her t-shirt on over the halter and wriggled into her jeans without taking off the belt. That sent a bolt of arousal through him, knowing what she was wearing under a thin layer of clothing.

But what was a little more arousal? He hardly noticed. His body was still teeming with it.

Before they headed upstairs he made a little adjustment, lifting her shirt and loosening the straps of the halter so her boobs were in a more normal configuration. He kissed the red marks on her sweet flesh, because he just couldn't resist before he dragged the cotton back down.

She winced.

"Sorry," he mumbled.

"It's okay," she said. My nipples are just…tender."

He nibbled his lip to hold back a smile. Because he'd been the one tenderizing them. "Are you ready to face the music?" She shot him a glare and smacked his shoulder, although this glare, unlike her other previous and numerous glares, held little heat.

Her words changed his temperature though. They sent a cold wind screaming through him. "Don't tell anyone, okay?"

"Don't tell anyone?"

"About us. This."

He nodded.

Because his lips wouldn't work.

Don't tell anyone.

Fuck.

They made their way up the stairs, Holt first. He opened the door to the great room and froze. Cam and Kristi. In a clinch. Great.

He cleared his throat and they sprang apart. Kristi turned away and quickly adjusted her blouse.

"Hey guys," he said.

"Oh, hey Holt." Cam dipped his head to hide his blush and shoved his fists in his pockets. Holt bit back a snort. At least he wasn't the only man in the house sporting wood. "We were wondering whose suitcase this was."

He glanced back at Bella, still on the stairs behind him. Her eyes widened and in them he read relief that they hadn't *opened* that suitcase. It was full of seriously kinky shit.

"Yeah. It's Bella's." He stepped aside to let her pass.

Kristi blanched. "Bella's here?"

"Right here." Bella's typical mask fell into place and she flounced into the room. "I should probably take this upstairs." She picked up the bag and toted it to the staircase. He should have helped her, but that would have given them away.

And she didn't want anyone to know about this. Not just yet. It was far too new. Too fragile, maybe.

Instead, he headed for the coffee pot and poured himself a cup, though he didn't really want it. He just wanted something to do. He took a sip and grimaced. It was cold.

"Have you been here long?" Cam asked, throwing himself into the recliner.

Holt grunted, noncommittally.

"It's a beautiful day." Kristi leaned against Cam's chair.

Holt remained where he was, behind the counter in the kitchen, willing his raging hard on to wane.

"I thought maybe I'd take the boat out," Cam said.

"That'd be nice." Again, Holt didn't give a shit.

When Kristi wandered into the kitchen, Holt turned away so she wouldn't notice his deformity. His still-raging hard on. For her sister. She poured a cup of coffee and then, after she tasted it, muttered, "Yuck." She put it in the microwave and punched some buttons. And as the microwave hummed away, she came to stand beside him.

He glanced down at her.

She smiled.

His cock throbbed.

It was awkward.

More so when Bella came bounding down the stairs and saw them standing next to each other in the kitchen. Her eyes narrowed.

Holt figured he'd better diffuse the situation and quickly. "So, who all's coming this weekend?" A stupid topic, but the situation did not call for brilliance. Merely desperation.

"Drew for sure," Cam said. "He and I are going to work on the boat." He tapped his lips with a finger. "And Emily and Kaitlin."

"Oh and Jamie," Kristi added.

"Nice." Yeah. Like it mattered. Only one person mattered, and she was glaring at him from across the room. It was going to be a bitch of a weekend, trying to stay across the room from her.

The microwave dinged and Kristi got her coffee, thankfully heading back to her boyfriend. Cam took the mug and tasted it.

God.

Already?

They'd only been dating a couple weeks and they were already sharing a coffee mug? That didn't bode well for Cam's bachelor status.

"Which room did you snag?"

Holt frowned at Cam. He knew why his friend was asking. The rule was, whoever showed up first got their choice of rooms. There were only two singles in the whole house.

Hell, that was why Holt had come early. To grab a private room. It was probably why Cam and Kristi had appeared today.

"I took Lane's." Hopefully he wouldn't be sleeping alone.

Cam blew out a breath and stood. "Okay. We'll take the one in the basement then."

Holt stilled. He quickly pulled up a mental image of the rec room as they'd left it. He had hidden all the toys. Hadn't he? He shot a look at Bella. The same thought was playing over her face.

As Cam went to get his and Kristi's suitcases, which they'd left by the door, Bella scurried over to the basement door and disappeared. He nearly laughed out loud. God, she was adorable.

And he loved that they shared a secret. As much as he wanted to bray it to the world.

She came back up a moment later, biting back a smile, and nodded to him. His sense that they were bound together in an unholy, though very satisfying alliance, swelled.

Well, not as satisfying as it could have been, if Cam and Kristi would have waited for the next ferry.

"What do you say we go to Darby's for lunch?" Cam asked and Holt nodded. Because hell, what else was there to do if he couldn't fuck Bella silly?

"Great," Kristi said. "We'll just get cleaned up and then we'll go."

Cam and Kristi headed downstairs. Holt watched them go. When they turned the corner into the rec room, he stormed over to Bella and yanked her into his arms.

"Wh-what are you doing?" she squeaked, though her breath came out in a little 'oof' when her chest hit his.

"This," he growled. And he kissed her.

It had only been ten minutes or so since he'd last touched her, but it had been far-too-fucking long.

He was gratified that her response was as feral, as hungry as his. Clearly her passion hadn't waned completely. He was glad to know it. Because she had come, several times today. He hadn't. His cock ached like hell.

"Wow." She pushed against him. Wiggled. "You are hard."

He was, but she was pushing against the egg. That reminded him. He pulled it out of his pocket and handed it to her, though he kept the remote. "Go clean this off, and then I want you to put it into your cunt."

She gaped at him. "What?"

"You heard me. And you better hurry. Cam and Kristi will be back any second."

"But we're going out for lunch, Holt. At Darby's."

"Yeah." He shot her an evil smile. "I know."

"Holt. It's a public place. You can't ask me to wear that there."

"Can't I?"

She fixated on the egg and paled. "But that would be torture."

"I'm in agony, Bella," he said. "Why should I be the only one suffering?"

CHAPTER NINE

The walk to Darby's Bar and Grill was agony. Pure aginy. Because as soon as she'd emerged from the bathroom with the evil egg tucked deep in her hoo-haw, Holt had reached into the pocket of his jacket and heinous vibrations had kicked into gear.

Oh, they were subtle and fluttery, as though the egg was on the lowest setting, but she felt every one. She was still slippery and wet from their earlier encounter, and, with each step down the dusty road, she had to contract her kegels to keep the damn thing in.

It was absolutely impossible to follow the conversation between the other three, though Kristi kept trying to drag her into it. Bella responded with one-word, clipped answers. She knew she was being rude—Kristi frowned at her more than once—but she really had no choice.

She glared at Holt as they reached the edge of town. He grinned.

Good thing he was on the other side of Cam, or she would have punched him.

They reached Darby's and Bella's steps slowed as a waft of cigarette smoke reached her. Hunger whipped through her. A group of young men lounged on the benches in front of the bar smoking up a storm. Damn she wanted a cigarette.

Holt must have caught her mooning at them—the cigarettes, that was—because the vibrator kicked up a notch. She stopped short. Winced.

"Bella. Are you all right?" Kristi asked.

It was all she could do not to snap back with something snotty. This wasn't Kristi's fault. Not in the least. Not the craving for nicotine. Certainly not the vibrating egg. She'd done both those things to herself.

"I'm okay," she muttered, and forced her feet to move.

The interior of the bar was dark. It always was. It took a moment for Bella's eyes to adjust. Honky-tonk music played on the jukebox. The crack of pool balls and laughter echoed through the room. She didn't glance at the pool hall. She couldn't. It would make her think of Holt, laying her down on the soft and scratchy felt and fucking her brains out.

Not that she had any brains left.

They turned left at the door into the dining room and headed for an empty booth. Most of the tables were empty. Even though it was summer, it was Thursday. The real crowd wouldn't show up until tomorrow.

Bella winced as she slid into the booth. She closed her eyes and focused on keeping that stupid egg from slipping out. Holt slid in next to her because Kristi and Cam took the other side. The guys flipped open the menus Charmaine brought and scanned the offerings. Though they knew them by heart.

Darby's was the only restaurant on the island, except for the little bakery on the corner, and if it wasn't breakfast, that place didn't count.

"What are you going to have?" Cam asked the table. It was a rhetorical question. Cam never cared what anyone else ordered. "I think I'll have a burger and a beer."

"Sounds good." Holt slapped his menu shut. "Bella? How about you? They're still serving eggs."

She glared at him.

"Eggs?" Kristi laughed. "Aren't you vegan?"

"I'll have a salad," Bella muttered. And, as an afterthought, "And a beer." She was going to need one.

Charmaine came by and took their orders, looking bright and cheerful in her Darby's Darlings apron. Charmaine would have been beautiful in a gunny sack. Bella tried not to growl at her when the waitress set her hand on Holt's shoulder as she chatted with them.

She was pretty sure they'd dated at one time. Or another.

Then again, if she growled at every woman Holt had ever dated, people would start thinking she was a rabid dog.

Something inside her shifted. Slipped. Nudged out. She paled. Her fingers tightened around her water glass.

"Bella." Kristi studied her with a worried expression. "Are you sure you're okay?"

"Yes," she hissed through her teeth. She turned and glared at Holt. "I have to use the bathroom."

He didn't move quickly enough, so she pushed him out of the booth so she could escape.

She heard him chuckle as she hop-skipped over to the ladies' room. And then the vibrator kicked up a notch.

Then two.

* * * * *

Bella was gone a long time.

Holt kept himself from shooting another glance over his shoulder at the back of the bar, but just barely. She'd better not have taken the egg out. He occupied himself thinking up scenarios where he punished her for that infraction while Cam and Kristi chatted about...whatever the hell they were chatting about. And then Kristi said something that snagged his attention. In a big way.

"Who's that guy Bella's talking to?"

His head whipped around like something from the *Exorcist*. He froze.

Bella was talking to a tall, blond guy by the jukebox. Even as he watched, the guy reached out and touched a finger to her breast. Okay, not her breast. The douche was tracing the logo on her t-shirt, but still, his hackles rose.

He reached in his pocket and flipped the vibrator on to max. Just to get her attention.

She jerked, and then whirled around to stare at him. He made a tiny movement with his head, but it should have shouted volumes. *"Come back here,"* it said. *"Now."*

"Oh, that's Ash Bristol." Holt heard a buzzing in the back of his head that might have been Cam talking.

"What?"

"Ash Bristol. He's our neighbor on the left." He raised a hand to wave. Holt glared at him. Because both Bella and Ash turned and headed back to the table.

"He's kinda cute," Kristi murmured. And then when Cam frowned at her, she added, "For Bella." She didn't have any response when Holt frowned at her.

But there was no more time for any frowning. Because Bella and Douche, um, Ash, reached the table just then.

"Scoot in," she said, waving her fingers and he did. But he immediately wished he hadn't.

"Why don't you join us, Ash," Cam offered. Cam was always offering shit like that. Why did he have to be so goddamn friendly?

Bella slid in next to Holt on the banquette and nudged his hip to make room for Ash to slip in as well.

Holt didn't like the way she was sandwiched between them. Mostly he didn't like the slice of bread on the other side of the sandwich.

He glared at Ash and their gazes locked over Bella's head. Holt bristled at the challenge in Ash's eyes. He reached in his pocket to turn the vibrator up and realized it was already on max. Still on max.

Bella's expression was wreathed in torment. *Shit*. With a grumble, more to himself than to anyone else at the table he turned it off. She collapsed against him in relief. "Thank you," she murmured. And then—because why should only one of them be stewing?—she added a whispered, "Sir."

Ash was a nice guy, and funny and Bella liked him, but she liked Holt's warmth to her right even more. Though she engaged in the riotous conversation and laughed and chatted and pretended to be super interested in every word that dripped from his mouth, she was aware of only one thing. The steamy, sexy man on her right.

The egg swam in her juices—literally swam in them. She could feel the dampness in her crotch and hoped to God it didn't look like she'd peed herself. Her body ached, throbbed with sexual tension. Because she was still wearing that halter, and her nipples were bare, they rubbed against her shirt incessantly. On the odd occasion when she moved wrong, they scraped against the table edge, swamping her with agony.

If she weren't here with her sister, she would drag Holt back into the bathroom, lock him in a stall and fuck him silly.

As it was, she didn't think she'd be getting his cock any time soon. Even when they headed back to the house, Kristi and Cam would still be hanging around for hours—Cam never went to bed before ten. They'd probably try to start a game of hearts.

And Bella was horny *now*.

She glared at Holt, annoyed that he was engrossed in a conversation with Ash and Cam about some stupid car race. It wasn't fair that she should be suffering like this, while he was chattering on like a NASCAR squirrel.

So she decided to make him suffer too.

She opened her silverware packet and dropped her napkin into her lap. One of the things she loved about Darby's was, even though it was a friendly, down-home kind of place, they still used cloth napkins.

Cloth napkins would serve her well at the moment.

She eased forward, only wincing a little when her nipples scraped against the table, and put her palm on his thigh.

He stilled. Stalled mid-word.

The other guys waited for him to finish what he was saying, expectantly. He never did. He cleared his throat and shook his head and muttered something vague.

With a curious glance, Cam picked up the thread of conversation and he and Ash were off again.

But Holt was silent. Still. Because her palm was creeping up his thigh.

When she found his cock, it was hard.

He skewered her with a dark frown as she traced its rigid bulk. Slipping his hand under the table, he captured her wrist, dragging it away from the danger zone. She wrestled it free.

He caught it again.

"Bella," he murmured in a warning tone.

"What, Holt?"

"Cut it out."

She smirked at him. "Why should I be the only one suffering?" He paled when he recognized his words from before. But then he leaned closer and whispered, "You're gonna pay for this tonight."

A slash of excitement whipped through her. She couldn't stop her wicked grin, which made him laugh, though it was a creaky laugh. A pained laugh.

She couldn't have been happier.

Because she was going to pay tonight.

She turned back to the conversation and her gaze tangled with Kristi's. She froze.

Shit.

Her sister had witnessed that entire exchange. She was now studying them both through narrowed eyes.

Shit.

Shit, shit, shit.

Kristi knew.

Their secret was out.

Apparently Holt had tipped to the fact Kristi knew, because just then he pretended to stretch and when he dropped his arm, it was around her shoulders. And then he pulled her against his side and kissed the shell of her ear.

"Tonight, Bella," he rumbled. "I can't fucking wait."

No. He couldn't wait.

Tonight was too far away.

His cock ached so bad it was difficult walking back to the house. With relentless determination, he focused on putting one foot in front of the other. It pissed the shit out of him that Ash had decided to come back with them. He walked beside Bella chatting her up. Every smile she gave the douche was a sword in Holt's gut.

So it also took relentless determination not to bash his face in.

He'd hoped Ash would veer off, down the dusty road to his own place when they reached his driveway. He didn't. He didn't veer.

Because Cam—damn his hide—invited him over for a beer.

Getting Bella away from her sister and Cam would have been difficult enough. But prying her away from a man determined to cleave to her side would be impossible.

Holt stewed. His thoughts churned. Sweat prickled on his brow, he thought so hard. There had to be a way. Some viable excuse to cut her from the herd.

He needed her. He needed to be in her.

Shit, he could practically taste the cum backing up.

As they all trouped through the back door, he grabbed her arm and held her back.

"Bella," he said. It was all he could manage and even at that, it was a feral growl.

Still, she seemed to understand. "I know, Holt," she whispered. He liked that there was a thread of desperation in her tone as well. "We'll figure something out."

But what that could possibly be was a mystery.

So they all got beers and sat around the table and chatted amiably, though how the others could miss the humming sexual tension, Holt couldn't fathom. Bella sat next to him, her heat, her scent wrapping around him like a seductive fist. Every time she moved or spoke or—for fuck's sake—breathed, his pulse leapt. He was about to lose it, just grab her and haul her off to his bedroom, when Kristi saved him.

She looked at the clock on the wall. "Wasn't there a hydroplane race today?"

Both Cam and Ash jolted to attention. Cam loved anything that had to do with boats. Kristi was a frickin' genius. "Shit. Yeah. What time did it start?"

"I think it's on now." Wait. Was that a mischievous grin Bella's sister just flashed at him? It was. Holt could have kissed her.

But Bella would kill him if he did.

The big screen was in the basement. They'd go down, make sure the race was really on, then find some excuse to leave. Popcorn. Or something.

"We should go watch it," he said. Just in case. Just in case anyone had any other stupid ideas. It was gratifying, that scrape of chairs in response to his suggestion. Everyone stood, except Bella.

"Aren't you coming?" Ash asked.

Holt's fingers curled. You know. So he wouldn't smash Ash's face or some shit like that.

Bella faked a yawn. It was a patently fake yawn. "No. I think I'll go take a nap. You guys enjoy the race."

It was clear Ash wanted to linger. Stay with Bella. Follow her like a horny pup. Fuck her maybe.

Holt slapped him on the shoulder, ostensibly pushing him toward the basement door. "This is gonna be a great race," he said. He kind of remembered there was a rivalry brewing between two of the boat captains. "What do you say to a bet?" As everyone filed down to the basement, Holt hung back, shooting a simmering scowl at Bella. "Don't start without me," he murmured. "And that's an order."

CHAPTER TEN

Bella winced as a bolt of lust whipped through her. Holy crap, she wanted him. It had been agony, holding in the damn egg. Her cunt was on freaking fire. She couldn't wait for Holt to sneak back upstairs, as surely that was what he was intending to do.

It took forever.

Forever.

For. Ever.

She sat there, stewing in her juices. Waiting. Aching. She was about to head down and see what was taking so damn long when the basement door creaked open. Her pulse leapt. She jumped to her feet, wincing as the egg wobbled inside her.

But it wasn't Holt's dark head that appeared. It was Ash.

Her belly plunged.

"Hey you," he said in a soft voice. It was a sultry tone. Shit. "I thought you were going to take a nap."

And he was coming to find her? She frowned. "In a bit." And then she added, just for something to say, "I'm not a fan of hydroplane races."

"Ah." She didn't like the way he said the word. The way his gaze drifted downward. She knew her nipples were hard. Hell, they'd been hard all day. Without the cloak of her bra, they were probably beacons to a hungry wolf like Ash. He stepped closer. She eased to the right, putting the table between them.

He followed.

Normally, having a gorgeous guy like Ash stalk her around a table would have been a thrill and a half. But as handsome as he was, and as buff and cocky and determined, he didn't move her in the slightest.

Well, he moved her. Around the table.

She felt like the secretary in a sixties spoof, avoiding a randy boss. She knew she couldn't outmaneuver him, especially with that ridiculous egg slipping the way it was, so she whirled and confronted him, thrusting out an arm to hold him back. Her palm landed on his chest.

Before Holt, she might have appreciated the definition of those pecs. Now, Ash's proximity, his determination, set her teeth on edge. "Hold on there, buster."

He blinked. Surprised, perhaps, at her tone.

Surprised, perhaps, that any woman would hold him off. The light in his eyes turned dark. "God," he rumbled. "You are so damn hot." He stepped closer and yanked her into his arms, ignoring her pathetic attempt to keep him at bay. "You nearly drove me crazy all through lunch with those come hither looks."

Come hither looks? What the fuck was he talking about?

He rubbed against her. His cock was hard. "Tell me you don't feel it."

Oh. She felt it.

"Ash, let me go." She pushed at his chest. He ignored her.

Well, not completely. He chuckled. As though her wriggling was a come on. "I've wanted to do this all afternoon." His head dipped and before she could protest, before she could wrench away, he kissed her.

Put his mouth on hers and shoved in his tongue.

And though her body was aching with lust, though her pussy was swimming with bubbling juice, it left her cold.

God damn it. He'd been distracted. One flipped boat and he'd let himself lose sight of the long game. And Ash had slipped away.

Holt knew exactly where he'd gone, what he had in mind. He leapt to his feet.

"Where are you going?" Cam asked.

Holt stared at his friend, willing his mind to work, willing his mouth to say something that made a modicum of sense. "Popcorn." It was all he could manage, but it seemed to work.

Cam nodded and turned back to the race.

Kristi sent him a speaking glance. He was pretty sure it said: Go save my sister. He bounded—bounded—up the stairs and burst into the great room.

His heart stopped. Breath snagged in his throat at the sight he beheld.

Bella. In another man's arms.

Oh, clearly she didn't want to be there, judging from the way she resisted, turning her head this way and that to avoid a marauding mouth. In that second, multiple emotions slammed through him. First and foremost, was rage. She was his woman. And another man had his filthy paws all over her.

Next up in the hierarchy of raging sentiment was extreme satisfaction that she had not submitted to Ash's kiss. He was a damn good looking guy, and suave and stinking rich to boot. According to Cam, Ash's dad was a billionaire. Still, all that money, all those muscles weren't enough to seduce her.

And finally, lust. Simply lust.

Although it was more than lust, really. It was a burning, seething desire to wrench her from the other man's embrace, bend her over the back of the sofa and lay claim. In her cunt. Multiple times. Again and again until she was so filled with him that every other man ceased to exist.

He'd never felt such an overwhelming sense of possession. It clawed at his soul, leaving painful scores.

"Bella." A sharp growl. A command.

They both froze.

Ash lifted his head and looked over his shoulder. Frowned.

Holt snapped his fingers. He really shouldn't have snapped his fingers, but he was in caveman mode.

Unholy glee suffused him as she disentangled herself from Ash's grip and padded to his side. She peered up at him with wide eyes. Damp eyes. Submissive eyes. He pulled her close, pressing a kiss on her forehead. "Good girl."

She curled up against him. Wrapping her arms around his waist. Goddamn, it felt good.

He fixed Ash with a steady gaze. A speaking gaze.

The douche studied the tableau they made, the commanding Dom and his obedient pet. Something, acknowledgement of defeat perhaps, flickered over his features. He blew out a breath. "Okay," he said. "I get it. Sorry if I misread the situation."

Holt grunted. He couldn't manage anything more. He jerked his head toward the basement.

Ash scrubbed his face with a palm and chuckled. Without another word, he headed back downstairs.

The door hadn't closed on his ass when Holt turned to Bella. Flames seared his veins at the expression on her face, all soft and dewy and yielding.

She smiled. "You handled that very we—"

He didn't let her finish. He couldn't. He silenced her with a kiss. Ravaged her. Jesus God. He needed to wipe the memory of Ash from her mouth. Needed to wipe the thought of any other man from her mind and heart and soul.

He backed her up against the wall and consumed her.

Her response was feral. She nearly crawled up his body. She fisted his hair and hooked her leg around his waist and rubbed against him like a cat in heat. Her moans were muffled, her grunts swallowed.

God he wanted her. Needed her.

He almost forgot where they were. He almost yanked her jeans off and plowed into her right there in the great room with Kristi and Cam and Ash just downstairs. But some remnant of sanity flared. What he wanted to do to her required no witnesses. Demanded privacy.

And the door to Lane's room had a deadbolt.

Bella nearly swooned when Holt lifted her into his arms as though she weighed nothing at all and headed for the bedroom. She wasn't hardly a swooning sort, but she wasn't herself at the moment. She didn't feel rebellious or bitter or snarky in the least.

That was certainly not independence surging in her veins. It was raw need. A need unlike anything she'd ever felt.

Normally she was the kind of woman who, when a man snapped his fingers at her, would snap them right off. But when Holt had snapped his fingers, all her intransigence had melted away, washed away, in a tsunami of lust.

It was as though she had devolved to her basest state. A woman in season. Hungry for her mate.

Thank God he'd whipped her into his arms like a conquering warrior and carried her to the bedroom. She couldn't have walked to save her life.

The door slammed behind them. The click of the lock rumbled through to her core.

"Holt…" she croaked. "The others…"

He stared down at her, reading her concern. They weren't far away. Though they were, no doubt, enraptured by the hydroplane races, they weren't far enough away.

"Then you'd better not make much noise." His expression warned her it might be difficult keeping quiet. He tossed her on the bed. She bounced. "Strip," he commanded, even as he ripped off his shirt. His features were tight, his nostrils flared. He toed off his boots and removed his jeans. Noticing her lounging on the bed enjoying the view, he barked, "Strip!"

She whipped into action, quickly divesting herself of her clothing. When she got to the leather halter she looked at him. His nod was infinitesimal, but she caught it and, with a sigh, slipped it off.

When her panties dropped, so did the egg. It had been hovering there on the brink of escape for a while.

He growled.

She paled. "I'm wet." As though that was excuse enough.

"On the bed," he ordered. "On your hands and knees."

She quickly complied. God, she wanted him. In. She peered at him through a curtain of unruly hair as he found a condom. He pulled off his briefs and his cock sprang free and—

Holy God.

Her mouth watered.

She'd wanted this. Needed it with a burning desperation for hours. She wiggled her ass. "Fuck me," she muttered, though it came out as a command. His features tightened even more as he stepped toward her. She could tell he was conflicted.

On the one hand, she had just issued a command for which she deserved punishment. On the other, he really wanted to fuck her.

He compromised with a smack to one upturned cheek. She squealed.

"Quiet," he snapped.

The bed dipped as he settled behind her, covering her. As though he couldn't resist, he smacked her ass again. And again.

She buried her face against her arm and moaned with each stinging slap. Heat suffused her. "Please. Please," she whimpered. "Please fuck me."

Apparently, that was what he'd been waiting for. If he had, indeed, been waiting.

He shoved in with one feral thrust.

Delight screamed through her soul as he filled her, hard and hot. Stretched her. Filled her. Fulfilled her.

"God, yes." An unrepentant wail.

He yanked out and plunged again. That orgasm, the one that had been hovering, tingling, teasing her since she'd first slipped that damn egg in, descended.

She saw stars. Dancing glittering brilliant stars.

"Yes. Yes. Yes," he chanted in time with each lunge. Each one sent new skeins of pleasure, ribbons of bliss slamming through to her soul.

She pushed back against him, hungry, frantic for more.

His pace increased. Became manic. Short. Hard. Fast.

Her nerves hummed as he stroked her sensitive inner folds, nudging, tormenting, delighting that bundle of sensation at her core. Another crisis, a larger disaster, loomed.

She sucked in a breath. Bore down. His cock swelled, surged, jerked.

A new sensation distracted her. A nudge against another sensitive orifice, one turned up so prettily for his attention. Her mind seized at the invasion of his thumb. Every muscle in her body clenched. He snarled something incomprehensible and drove deeper. Into her cunt. Into her ass.

Heaven and hell coalesced into a blinding miasma of excruciating rapture. She might have lost consciousness for a second, so intense was this pleasure. Fortunately, her body did not need her mind. Her body did not need thought or logic or any rational conjecture.

It took flight. On its own.

But no. He was there. With her.

Soaring, flying, escaping.

Liberated.

Free.

Nothing else mattered. Not her failing business or her family issues or the fact that she always felt so fucking alone in the universe.

Because he was there. With her. In her. Holding her.

Completing her.

It was too scary to talk, once she regained her sanity, so she curled up against him, where he'd collapsed, chest heaving, and nuzzled into him. He wrapped his arms around her and held her tight. Too tightly, almost, but she didn't wiggle away as she might have once done.

She didn't want to wiggle away. She wanted to stay. Right here. Forever, maybe.

Yeah. Fucking scary.

Because this was Holt Lamm.

The guy who had a different girlfriend every week. Sometimes more than one at a time.

At any moment, he could be done with her. And on to the next best thing.

She peeped up at his face. Stilled when she found him staring at her, his lips tight, nostrils flared.

He opened his mouth to say something and she steeled her spine. She always hated that moment. The moment *after* where someone felt like they had to say something and usually ruined everything.

But he didn't say anything.

He yanked her closer and kissed her. A feral open-mouthed kiss that stated, without equivocation, he was far from done with her.

That was perfect.

Holt didn't want to let her go. Not ever. But he had to. At some point.

No doubt Cam would come hunting for his popcorn soon.

He should get up. Go make it.

Instead, he gently eased a lock of hair from her cheek and tucked it behind her ear. God, she was beautiful. Always, really, but especially like this. With that light of absolute satisfaction in her eyes.

He pressed his lips to her forehead. Her fluttering lashes. The tip of her nose.

"I'm still coming to your room tonight," he warned. Loved that she chuckled.

"You'd better."

"Cam and Kristi are sleeping in the basement."

She shot a look at him, her brow knit.

"And you're upstairs."

Her confusion deepened.

"That's two floors between us. You can beg as loudly as you'd like."

Oh yeah. That got her. Her pupils dilated. Lips parted. She shivered.

"I-I'm not wearing that egg again." She said it like a question. A plea.

"Not today, at least." He bit back a grin at her horrified expression. "Everyone will be here tomorrow," he added, just for good measure. "Just think how much fun I can have tormenting you."

"Beast." She smacked him on the shoulder, but without any real heat. Damn he liked her like this, all compliant and soft and docile in his arms. He loved when she snapped at him too, and resisted and pushed back. He loved that she was her own woman. But he loved that he could bring her to heel.

That she *allowed* him to bring her to heel.

She had no idea. No clue how much power she had over him. He hadn't even realized until the moment he'd seen her in Ash's arms. It had hit him like a ton of bricks. This was what he'd wanted. She was the one he'd been searching for.

He'd always been attracted to her, drawn to her on a visceral level. But he'd always sensed a wall in her. A bone deep repudiation of him and everything he stood for. He should have known she'd built that wall with bricks of fear. Fear of opening up to the simmering desire within.

She didn't like feeling vulnerable. He knew she'd been hurt, and hurt bad, in the past. But that was her fault. For picking the wrong guys. He would never hurt her. This, he vowed.

He would never hurt her. Never make her regret opening up to him, allowing him in.

"I should probably go make popcorn."

She snorted a laugh. "Why?"

He cracked a grin. Yeah. Cracked it. It was an effort. Nothing about this sense of obligation, this burning intent was amusing. "It was my excuse for leaving the basement."

"Okay." She blew out a breath and pulled away, casting about for her clothes. He couldn't stop his hand from reaching out, stop his fingers from trickling down her bare back. Her skin was smooth. Warm.

She looked at him over her shoulder. Smiled.

His heart thudded so hard he felt it in his bones.

Love wasn't a word he ever said. It wasn't an emotion he contemplated. But now, at this moment, it flooded through him, swamping his soul.

Funny how it ached like that.

Funny how it made him—the heartless Dominant who went through women like condoms in a whorehouse—feel vulnerable. Like a helpless boy.

She could crush him like a bug.

The thought scared him to death.

CHAPTER ELEVEN

An unaccountable lightness filled Bella's heart as she and Holt puttered in the kitchen making popcorn. It was silly to feel this way, she told herself. But she couldn't make it go away.

And she didn't want to.

Every once in a while their gazes would tangle and they'd smile and then, maybe, he'd kiss her.

Or she'd kiss him.

It took a while to make the popcorn, because they kept forgetting what they were doing. Needless to say, the race was over by the time it was ready. So, when Cam and Kristi clomped up the stairs—without Ash, who had, for some reason, left without collecting on the bet he'd won—they all sat around the table and ate it from the bowl.

Of course Kristi suggested a game of Hearts. Bella didn't roll her eyes, but just barely. She hated Hearts. She always had. There was something just wrong about trying to not get any points. It went against the grain.

So, of course, Bella lost. Dismally.

But it passed the time. Until tonight.

She kept thinking about it, flicking looks at Holt, who seemed engrossed in the game. What adventures would the evening hold? Would it be hard, hot sex, a frantic conflagration like this afternoon? Or something slower? Softer? Gentler?

He glanced at her and she read his expression. No. Definitely not gentle. She bit back a smile, and then gave up and let the grin blossom on her face.

Gentle was overrated.

They would be two floors away from her sister and Cam. Maybe he would smack her bottom again. She'd really liked that. Hell, she'd liked all of it. She couldn't believe he'd stuck his finger in her pucker. That had blown her mind.

Anal sex was not on her bucket list, but apparently a little ass play might be in order.

She thought she knew herself, but in the course of a couple days, Holt had shown her truths she'd never even suspected.

Then again, everything he did surprised her.

Which also surprised her.

Because she thought she'd known him, inside out and backwards as well.

She'd been wrong.

There was more to Holt Lamm than she ever suspected. Somehow, through these few brief encounters, she'd caught a glimpse of the real man. The man lurking beneath his brash, blasé exterior.

She cloaked her own vulnerability beneath a brittle mask. She'd never imagined he had done the same.

As they played, they chatted and while Bella had never had a lot of patience for small talk, she enjoyed this. She enjoyed getting to know him better.

Oh, Kristi and Cam said a bunch of stuff, but all that went in one ear and out the other. She focused on Holt.

Yeah, he said when Cam asked. *His business was doing well. There was a surge in construction and everyone needed architects.* She'd known he was an architect, somewhere in the back of her brain, but she hadn't actually thought about it. When she asked what architects actually did, he told her, in detail, rambling on about design and blueprints and load-bearing walls. She soaked it all in like a sponge.

Cam tried to start talking about writing computer code, but Bella interrupted and asked more questions of Holt. Like, how did they earthquake-proof a structure? Why were houses always framed with wood? And what the heck was with the current trend of designing buildings to look like they were leaning sideways?

Her interrogation went on through dinner, though it drifted from his work to his hobbies—fishing and hiking, both of which she enjoyed—and his favorite place for brunch, a little lodge perched on the brink of the raging Snoqualmie Falls.

And he had a cat.

Who knew?

Who the fuck would ever have guessed that?

Then he turned the tables. Asked about her life, her work. And she clammed up.

She must have been pretty obvious about it because when her jaw clamped shut, Kristi's eyes narrowed on her.

"Yeah," she said. "How are things going with your shop Bella?"

The question was tentative and, Bella suspected, sincere. That didn't make it any less painful.

Bella poked a Brussels sprout with her fork. It deserved it. She despised Brussels sprouts.

"Great," she gusted. "Fabulous."

"That's good to hear," Cam said. Of course he would take her at face value. Cam took everything at face value. "I read an article yesterday that retail sales were taking a nose dive locally."

She glared at him. "All right. Fine. It's going terribly." She had no idea why she said it. She certainly didn't want any of them to know. "I'm about a two months away from filing bankruptcy."

"Oh Bella!" She hated pity from Kristi. Or maybe not.

"Yeah. It sucks." She forced a smile, but it was bitter at best. "Most likely, I'll be looking for a job soon. I could probably make a Latte." Maybe. If she tried really hard to silence the screaming in her soul.

The expression on her sister's face firmed. It became almost…warlike. Very unlike Kristi. "No. We'll figure this out. We'll figure out a way to bring in more customers. What kind of marketing plan do you have?"

Bella blinked. "Marketing plan?" She'd opened the shop because it was risqué and rebellious…and shit.

Kristi blew out a breath. Which might have held a tinge of frustration. "Okay. Tara's coming tomorrow. We'll buttonhole her and gets some ideas for you. She helped Lucy and me when we opened Beanie's. She's brilliant."

"Her bakery is doing great," Cam added, nodding like a bobble head doll. "And bakeries have one of the highest rates of failure of all businesses."

"You need a hook." Kristi tapped her lips. "You need something that's going to grab people's attention."

"Sex doesn't grab their attention?"

But Kristi was ignoring her. She was off. That was the thing about Kristi. When she took on a challenge, she took it on wholeheartedly. "Contests are great for bringing back repeat customers. And a loyalty program. Do you have one of those?"

"A punch card for dildos?"

"And media coverage. I bet if we came up with some clever campaign, something different, unique, off the wall, that would garner some coverage…" She babbled on but Bella had ceased to listen. She was too *verklempt*. Too close to bursting into tears.

She and Kristi had been at odds for years. Constant rivals. Almost enemies. But here she was, taking up the banner, for Bella. After every nasty thing Bella had ever said or done. It was kind of humbling.

As uncomfortable as this feeling was, she liked it.

She dashed away a tear and glanced at Holt. He was watching her with a steady gaze. His lips quirked. And warmth suffused her.

It had been a long, long time since she'd felt this embraced. This defended. This safe.

As though, after an eternity in an inhospitable land, she had finally returned home.

"You know," Holt said as he handed Bella a skillet to dry. They'd lost the coin toss and been saddled with cleaning up after dinner. Though he didn't feel as if he'd lost anything at all. Cam and Kristi had gone out on the deck and he had Bella all to himself. "I could probably send some customers your way."

Hell. Could he. He had lots of connections in the BDSM community. One of his friends ran a club and had been toying with the idea of offering select items for sale. He might be open to the idea of letting Bella handle that for him.

She didn't respond. Didn't look at him, but he saw her smile.

He wrapped his arm around her shoulders, though he was sudsy. "We'll get you back on track, Bell," he said.

She whipped around. "What did you call me?"

"Bell?"

Her brow arched with exquisite scorn. At least, he thought it was scorn, but then she said, in a soft, musing tone, "A nickname? Already, Lamm? Moving pretty fast, aren't we?"

He chuckled, relieved that she was in a playful mood. It boded well for tonight. "Hardly a nickname. More of a truncation of your name."

Now both brows shot up. "*A truncation of my name?* Seriously?"

"I could call you *Buh.*"

"I wouldn't recommend it." She paused and flicked him a wicked grin. "*Lambchop.*"

"Really? Lambchop? Is that the best you can do?"

"Beats douche nozzle."

He chuckled. It did. "If I was going to give you a nickname, it would probably be something like Hot Cross Buns."

She made a face.

"Hot, because you're hot. Cross, well, because it's your name. Also, you're always cross—"

She smacked him with the towel. "I am not!"

"And buns, because I'm aching to paddle them."

Yeah. That shut her up. She nibbled her lush lower lip. "You are?"

"Mmm hmm. Too bad you didn't have a paddle in your sex suitcase."

"It isn't a sex suitcase." She dropped to a whisper, halfway through the adamant declaration, because the slider opened and Cam and Kristi came into the room talking softly to each other. Apparently the sun had finally set.

The sun set late during the summer in the Pacific Northwest. It was nearly nine pm. It was all Holt could do not to snap, "Go to bed," to his friends. Instead he dipped his head and murmured, "I saw some other interesting items I could use."

The flogger was still under the sofa cushions in the basement—probably lost to him tonight because he didn't want to take the chance of having Kristi and Cam see him retrieve it. But he'd seen a pair of rhinestone studded flip flops in her suitcase. Those would do in a pinch.

He was nothing if not flexible.

After they'd loaded dishes in the dishwasher, and all the pots and pans were piled in the rack, they hung out together in the great room, listening to music and talking. Cam and Kristi sat together on the loveseat while Bella and Holt sat side by side on the sofa. She loved the weight of his arm over her shoulders.

It was relaxing. It was congenial. It was nice.

She felt cosseted and warm and drowsy.

But when Kristi yawned, everything in her perked up.

That might have had something to do with Holt's sudden tension. "It's getting late," he murmured.

"Is it?"

Damn Cam.

"It is." Kristi yawned again, but Bella could tell it was a fake yawn. She patted Cam's thigh. "We should probably go to bed."

"But it's not so late…" Cam trailed off when he caught Kristi's heavy-lidded expression. He jumped up from the sofa. "Yeah. Man. Am I beat." He stretched hugely.

Again, totally fake. Neither of them could act worth a shit.

Bella couldn't have cared less.

"Well, sleep tight," Kristi said as she took Cam's hand and led him to the basement door.

"You too," Holt responded.

Bella didn't understand the thread of amusement in his voice. She glanced up at him. "What?" she asked.

His lips quirked. "She said 'sleep tight.'"

"So?"

"So…I was just thinking about those restraints in your suitcase."

Bella froze. Her pulse surged. Her womb clenched.

All of a sudden, the casual, laidback energy between them turned into an electric hum.

"You, um, you weren't thinking of tying me up, were you?"

He threaded his fingers through her hair. "Of course I was. I haven't stopped thinking about it since I laid eyes on those straps. But..." He kissed her. Hard on the mouth. "I'll only do it if you beg me to."

She snorted. Which was awkward. He was still kissing her, after all. "If I beg you to?"

"Mmm hmm."

"What makes you think I'm going to beg you to?" Though the prospect didn't horrify her the way it had when they'd first discussed it. That, in itself, should have horrified her.

"You'll beg because you want it."

"I do?"

"Yes, Bella. Deep down, you want it. You crave that sense of helplessness."

She frowned at him. "I do?"

"Yep. Let me tell you what it would be like." He tucked her back into his arms, against his chest and stroked her back as he spoke. "First, your punishment."

"My punishment?"

"Did you forget I owed you one?"

"For what?"

"The egg."

She grunted. Yeah. She'd dropped the egg. Though she'd had good reason. Although she'd come to realize good reason hardly counted in his games.

"I'm going to have you bend over, completely naked, and hold onto your ankles while I work you over. Then, once your ass is nice and red, you'll stand. I'll command you to lace your fingers behind your neck and hold still while I continue..."

"Continue?"

"Mmm hmm. There are other things that need paddling." His palm drifted to her heated crotch. He rubbed her clit through the seam of her jeans. She set her teeth together to hold back a groan. *Damn. Damn, damn.*

"When I feel you've been punished sufficiently, I'm going to tie you to the bed—"

"You are?"

"Once you beg me, of course. Once you beg me, I'll tie you to the bed and tease you."

"T-tease me?"

"Yes. And you'll be completely helpless. At my mercy."

She shivered. Why this talk was turning her on, she had no idea.

"I'll start with your nipples, which will be sore, tender—"

"They will be?"

"Mmm hmm." His light touch skated over her nape, down her arm, around to scrape over a swollen crest. His other hand was still nested in the crux of her thighs. He gave her a dual pinch. She shuddered. "I'll be paddling them too. Like I did this morning."

She swallowed. "Uh huh."

"And then I'll make my way down your body. Tickling you a little. You are ticklish, aren't you my Bell?"

Her pulse lurched. In her clit.

"Then, I'll torment you." Hell. He was tormenting her now. "I'll eat your pussy. Slowly. Diligently. Until I drive you crazy. Until you're thrashing and moaning and pleading for mercy. But I won't let you come."

"You-you won't?"

"No. You'll be tugging against the restraints. Wild. Crazed. Mad with lust and I'll keep teasing you. I might slip a finger inside, but it will be just now and again, and leave you aching for more."

Shit. She was aching for more now. And he hadn't even started.

Or maybe he had.

"And then, if you're very good, if you're obedient and do everything I ask, with no hesitation, I might fuck you." He ended on a whisper, as though he were as wrapped in the fantasy as she. But...

"Holt?"

"Hmm?"

"What if..."

"Yes?"

"What if I ask you to untie me?"

"I will." He cupped her cheeks and tipped her head and stared into her eyes. "Immediately."

"Do you promise?"

"Yes." A sigh. On a breath. As he kissed her gently, softly, reverently. "I promise."

It was a rarity, a man who kept his promises.

But Bella didn't ask to be released from her bonds until they were both covered in sweat and exhausted and utterly sated.

He'd been right.

She had loved being tied, helpless, in those devious restraints as he worked her over, finding new places to touch, tease, torment. Places she'd never thought of as erotic before. Now every part of her body was an erogenous zone, from the backs of her knees to the small of her back to the little knob on the side of her foot.

He'd kissed, licked, explored her—everywhere.

When she could take it no more, when her wails were rising to air-horn proportions, he rearranged her restraints. Just a hook here, a clasp there, splaying her open. And he fucked her.

There was something about it that released a wild woman within her. The restriction of her bonds, the dominion he exerted over her as he slid in and out at his own pace, taking her slowly, deliberately, with excruciating precision. She had no control over anything, but absolute control over everything.

She'd never felt so completely...*possessed.*

And her orgasm? It had been sublime.

It seemed illogical, incomprehensible, that each one could get better, stronger, more profound. But they did.

After the passion waned, he released her and kissed the little marks on her wrists and ankles and legs. Then he gently turned her over and caressed her still-burning ass. With a practiced hand, he soothed her, brought her back into the world.

A world that, all of a sudden, didn't seem so bleak.

They fell asleep in each others' arms, wrapped together in a bed that was far too small for both of them.

They awoke sometime in the night and made love again, gently, tenderly. This time she explored him—everywhere. Until they were wreathed in sighs and whispers and deep-throated moans.

She loved that she could make him beg too.

CHAPTER TWELVE

The morning was half gone when Holt finally woke up. Though his neck ached from sleeping on his side all night—or half of it, as the case may have been—Holt didn't move. He liked the feel of Bella's bare ass pressed against his cock far too much.

He liked everything about her. Her soft curves, her grumpy frowns, her snarls. Especially in bed.

He nearly laughed at the thought, but didn't. He didn't want to wake her.

She'd been amazing last night, submitting to his every command and then taking it a step further. The feel of her lips wrapped around his dick had been un-fucking-believable.

Despite his determination not to disturb her, his arms tightened and she stirred. She rolled over slowly to face him.

Ah. She was awake.

Her eyes were like dark pools, a stunning azure, wreathed in thick black lashes. She studied him without saying a word, and then she reached up and stroked his cheek. "Fuzz," she commented.

He watched her lips move, and, because he couldn't not, kissed her.

"Morning," he said. His voice was scratchy. Probably on account of all the howling and growling he'd done last night, fisting the sheets as she fisted his shaft, lapped around his sensitive head then drew him deep into her—

Yeah. He was hard again.

She smiled as his cock nudged her hip. "Morning Lambchop."

He grimaced through a grin. "Don't call me that. I'm not a sock puppet."

"You could be my sock puppet." She stilled as the words slipped out. Something flickered across her expression. It looked like retreat.

He knew Bella. She wasn't a runner, but she did close up when things got a little too intimate. A little too raw.

Hell no.

She wasn't retreating. He couldn't allow it.

He couldn't bear to lose her now, not even a bit of her. They'd come too far.

Last night had been everything he'd ever dreamed of. He wanted nothing more than a lifetime of "last nights."

He yanked her against him and kissed her again. She allowed it, but pulled away too soon.

"We should get dressed." She said it breezily, though he noticed the tiny lines around her mouth.

"No, Bella. We should talk."

She froze, halfway out of bed, and then sat by his side. He shifted onto his back. Cracked his neck to ease the tightness.

"What-what do you want to talk about?"

"Us. This. I think we should." Hell, everyone would be arriving today. There wouldn't be much chance for a private chat. Especially once all the girls arrived. They were like a flock of birds when they were all together, chirping away, flying in formation. It would be the guys on one side of the room talking about sports or cars and the girls on the other talking about whatever it was they talked about. Make up. Or shoes.

That's the way it always was.

He didn't want things to be the way they'd always been between them. Not anymore.

"Okay." She folded her hands, making her look like a schoolgirl waiting for the professor's instruction.

He shuttled that image away. If he went in that direction, they'd never get to talking.

"Bella." He toyed with the ends of her long hair, unsure what to say. He was tempted to let his body say it for him, but that was the coward's way out. Besides, she might misunderstand. Might miss the depth of his meaning. Better to just come out and say it. "I…like this."

Damn. Like wasn't the word he meant.

But he didn't dare use *that* word. Not yet. Too soon. He didn't want to scare her off.

She swallowed. Glanced at him, though he could tell it was an effort for her to hold his gaze. "I…like it too."

"Even the part where I tied you up?"

Her expression flickered.

Shit. He shouldn't have joked. This was no joking matter.

He cleared his throat and began again. "I would really like to continue…exploring…things."

Her lips tweaked. Shyly. "Even the part where I tie *you* up?"

His heart stopped. Not because he was turned on at the thought—though he was, maybe, a little—but because of the warmth, the openness, the acceptance in her eyes. It was what he wanted to see. What he needed to see.

"Wherever it takes us." His voice cracked a little. "I've always…had a…thing for you." He stroked her shoulder, her back, her hip. She edged closer.

"See, I was sure you had a thing for Kristi." She blew out a breath and studied her laced fingers. "I saw you kiss her, you know."

He blanched. "You saw me kiss her?"

"Last month. The last time we were all here together."

Oh. Crap.

He forced a laugh. "Did you see Cam deck me?"

"What?"

"Oh, yeah. Right in the kisser. I was drunk. I shouldn't have done it."

"You shouldn't have done it because you were drunk? Or you shouldn't have done it, period?"

"Period. She wasn't the one I wanted to kiss, anyway."

"She wasn't?"

"No." He drew her closer. "But I gave up on you long ago. Figured I'd never have a chance."

She sighed. Smiled. A little. "I am difficult."

"You…can be. But it wasn't that." He winked. "I kind of like that."

"Then why?"

The words caught in his throat. God, it was hard to say. "I always…had the sense you disliked me." It had torn him up, that hint of distain in her expression.

"I disliked seeing you with other women. Always. Incessantly."

Her vulnerability gored him, but he loved that she trusted enough to share it with him. He swore to himself, then and there, he would never, ever let her down. He put his palm over his heart. "As long as we are together Bella, and this I swear, I will not so much as look at another woman."

She issued a snort of disbelief. "You have to look at them. Or you'll bump into them."

"Do I have your permission to look at them then?" He batted his lashes. "You know. So I won't bump into them?"

Her lips worked. "D-do you require my permission?"

"Yes, Bella." Hell. His heart required her permission to beat, if she only knew it. He cleared his throat. "If you so command it, darling, I will close my eyes and stumble around, feeling my way like a blind man who's lost his cane."

She thought about this for a moment, tapping on her lower lip. The minx. "No," she said after a long, long while. "I think you should look where you're going." He collapsed in mock relief and she grinned. "Because God only knows where those flailing hands might land."

He snorted a laugh. "Boobs." A prediction, but not really.

She waggled her finger at him. "No boobs for you. Only these boobs." She thrust them forward.

"Yes ma'am." He levered up and took advantage of the bounty, drawing a berry-ripe nipple into his mouth until she threw back her head and raked his scalp with needy claws.

He loved playing with her. The teasing and joking…and this. She tasted delicious.

And his cock was hard.

He eased her down by his side and focused on the soft bounty of her breasts, cupping and exploring and tormenting himself at length. He wanted more. So much more.

But their conversation wasn't over.

"Holt?"

"Hmm?"

"So while we, ah, explore this, we agree to be monogamous?" Why she said it as a question was a mystery. There was no doubt whatsoever in his mind.

"Mmm hmm." He lifted his head as a thought struck him. "And no other guys for you. Right?"

She made a face. "As if."

He narrowed his eyes. "Ash was panting over you hot and heavy."

"Pfft." She flicked her hand dismissively. "His hair is too short."

Holt growled at the back of his throat. "A man can grow his hair."

"Too blond. Like, surfer dude much?"

"A guy can dye his hair."

"All right. Fine. Do you know what's wrong with Ash?"

"What?" He anticipated her answer on bated breath. And damn. Was it a good answer.

"He's not you. That's what's wrong with Ash. There's nobody quite like Holt Lamm." She pulled his head down for another kiss. And then, just before their lips met, whispered, "Chop."

The kiss lasted for a long time, and left them both breathless. When Bella was a limp noodle in his arms, pliable and subdued, as he held her and idly stroked her hair, he decided to tackle the other issue that had been bugging him.

"And Bella?"

"Mmm?"

"The smoking?"

She leaned up on an elbow and looked down at him. "Yeah?"

"That has to stop."

"I know." She frowned. "But I warn you, I might get cranky."

His expression made it clear…no one would probably notice the difference. "I know it won't be easy, but sweetheart, if you ever want a cigarette, just let me know." He bit back a grin. "I'd be happy to give you something else to suck on."

"Really?" She arched a brow. "Because I kind of want a cigarette now."

Which was exactly what he was hoping she'd say.

EPILOUGE
Twenty-One Days Later

"Are you okay?" Holt's breath skated over Bella's cheek, sending a shiver through her. She arched her back and readjusted her arm. It was starting to ache. He'd had her tied in this position for a while. Everything ached. Her nipples, her clit, her ass. Especially her ass.

Was she okay?

She was wonderful.

"Yes Sir."

"Good girl." His fingers played along her spine and she sighed. Warmth dribbled through her. Odd how this had happened. She was never happier than she was with him. And her ass hurt.

Holt was the most creative lover she'd ever known. The sexiest man. The most tender heart. He'd shown her that, over and over again in the past few weeks. Shown her how much he cared. Shown her what she'd been missing.

She didn't want to miss it any more.

Every time with him had been phenomenal, whether it was sweet and sexy or kinky as hell. She'd particularly loved his training sessions.

She wanted this every day. Always. She wanted to be his.

Oh, she was still a brat. He would probably never train that out of her. And she suspected he wouldn't want to.

Holt loved her for who she was.

And she loved him.

Completely.

"How are those cravings, darling?"

Bella blinked as his soft question wrenched her from her dreamy reverie. She nibbled at her lower lip. "Cravings?"she asked, though she knew what he was talking about.

He chuckled. "You haven't mentioned cigarettes in a while."

It had been twenty one days since her last cigarette. Twenty one days, three hours and seventeen minutes. And oddly enough, she didn't want one. Hadn't wanted one for days. Not even when he mentioned them.

Glancing over her shoulder, she fixated meaningfully on his crotch. "Oh," she quipped, "does someone need a blowjob?" She was careful to use a playful, pouty voice and though a light flared in his eyes, his expression darkened.

"What did I tell you about that attitude, missy?"

She loved the way his low voice rumbled around her. Loved the skitter of excitement dancing through her veins. "Sorry."

She wasn't. Not really. And he knew it.

He blew out a heavy sigh, but she caught the twitch of his lips. Yeah. He loved it when she was a brat. "Bella, Bella, Bella," he tsked.

"Holt, Holt, Holt."

Again, a little too much attitude.

The crack of the lash caught her by surprise and she jumped with a squeal. She didn't jump much, because her bonds were fairly tight.

"I think we're ready to start again," he said and she bit back a smile.

Because she was. She was very ready.

AN EXCERPT FROM

HEART OF ASH
Book 4 in the Tryst Island Series

"Are you ready for our mystery date?"

"And how. Where are we going?" he asked as he held the door for her.

Her wicked expression shocked him to the core. "We're staying here."

Gooseflesh prickled on his nape. He blinked at her. Several times. "Alone?" Was that a hint of panic in his voice? Definitely. Panic.

He didn't think he could do that. Be alone with her and keep his hands to himself. It had been way too long since he'd had her.

A month was far too long.

He was weak. Vulnerable.

Hungry.

"Emily, I don't think you understand—"

She cut him off. "Did you mean what you said? About making it up to me?"

"I did. I've been trying…" But hell. How was he supposed to control himself in her living room? Her kitchen? Her freaking foyer?

Doubt flickered over her expression. He hated it, so he forced a smile. "Yes. Yes. Emily. I meant it."

"Anything I want?"

He gulped. "Anything."

Her response was a gamine grin. How a woman with such a sweet innocent mien could appear so evil was beyond him.

"Then we're having dinner here."

His heart ker-chunked. They were utterly alone.

And they would not be disturbed.

Holt would not be glaring at them from across the room.

There would be no crowds to shoulder through. No waiters or waitresses to interrupt with an offer of coffee.

How on earth was he going to survive this?

He swallowed heavily. And nodded. "Okay."

As she showed him into the dining room, where an elegant, romantic, table was set, he took in the details of her home. While it wasn't a large house, it was perched on a hill overlooking Seattle. The décor was classy, elegant, simple. Chopin played in the background, masking the muted barking of her neighbor's dogs.

The view from her bay window was stunning, the city lights reflecting off the waters of the Sound.

It was so…her.

Perfect for a girl who liked to stare at water.

Despite his trepidation, dinner was delightful. They talked and laughed through the meal, both of them completely at ease. Well, perhaps not completely.

Every once in a while he would remember how alone they were. How close she was, how very eager she was, the lilt of her eyes when she came…and a simmering unrest would ferment in his bowels.

She seemed similarly effected…every once in a while. She would shoot him a glance and a flush would creep up her cheeks and she would lower her lashes and nibble her lower lip and, occasionally, lace her fingers together. He assumed it was nervousness.

Hell, he was nervous.

He didn't seem to have any trouble devouring the meal though, a delicious standing roast with Yorkshire Pudding. And then she brought out an incredible burnt crème. If he hadn't thought her the perfect woman before, he surely did now.

When he'd finished the last bite, he tossed his napkin on the table, gusted a sigh and looked at her. And froze.

Her expression made him restless.

"Emily?"

"Did you enjoy your dinner, Ash?" A shy smile.

"Yes."

"Are you ready for…dessert?"

He glanced at the burnt crème. Or what remained of the custard he'd inhaled.

"I…ah… Yes?"

A flush crept up her cheeks. Her lashes fluttered. She cleared her throat. "Good. Because there is…something I'd like to try."

The tone of her voice set his nerves humming.

"Wh-what is it?"

"Do you trust me?"

He stared at her. Did he trust her? Yes. But she was a woman scorned. God only knew what she had in mind. And he had invited her to punish him…

Hell. It didn't matter, did it? He'd agree to anything she offered. Anything at all to be with her.

"Yes."

"Excellent." The glint in her eye sent a raging wildfire through him. And then his heart skittered to a halt. Because she pulled out a pair of handcuffs.

Oh, they were covered with fur and all pink and shit, but they scared him to death.

Holy God.

His pulse pounded. Sweat beaded his brow. His cock rose.

"What-what are those for?"

"I think you know."

Shit. He did.

He wasn't sure if he should be excited as hell—or run.

ABOUT THE AUTHOR

Her Royal Hotness, Sabrina York, writes naked erotic fiction for fans who like it hot, hard and balls-to-the-wall, and erotic romance and fantasy for readers who prefer a slow burn to passion.

An award winning author of hot, humorous stories for smart and sexy readers, her titles range from sweet & sexy erotic romance to BDSM to erotic horror. Connect with her on twitter @sabrina_york, on Facebook or on Pintrest. Check out Sabrina's books and read an excerpt Amazon or wherever e-books are sold. Visit her webpage at www.sabrinayork.com to check out her books, excerpts and contests. Don't forget to enter to win the royal tiara!

BOOKS BY SABRINA YORK

Adam's Obsession (Erotic Contemporary, Ellora's Cave)
Dark Duke (Erotic Regency, Ellora's Cave)
Brigand (Erotic Regency, Ellora's Cave)
Dark Fancy (Erotic Regency, Ellora's Cave)
Devlin's Dare: A Tryst Island Erotic Romance (Erotic Contemporary)
Dragonfly Kisses: A Tryst Island Erotic Romance (Erotic Contemporary)
Extreme Couponing (Erotic Contemporary, Ellora's Cave)
Fierce (One Night Stand, Decadent Press)
Five Alarm Fire (Erotic Contemporary for the High Octane Heroes Anthology, Cleis Press)
Folly (Erotic Regency, Ellora's Cave)
Heart of Ash: A Tryst Island Erotic Romance (Erotic Contemporary)
Lust Eternal (Erotic Fantasy, Ellora's Cave)
Pushing Her Buttons (Erotic Contemporary, Ellora's Cave)
Making Over Maris (Erotic Contemporary, Ellora's Cave)
Man Hungry (Erotic Contemporary, Ellora's Cave)
Rebound: A Tryst Island Erotic Romance (Erotic Contemporary)
Rising Green (Erotic Horror, Ellora's Cave)
Saving Charlotte (Erotic Contemporary for the Smokin' Hot Firemen Anthology, Cleis Press)
Smoking Holt: A Tryst Island Erotic Romance (Erotic Contemporary)
Training Tess (Erotic Contemporary, Ellora's Cave)
Trickery (Erotic Contemporary with Magical Elements, Ellora's Cave)
Tristan's Temptation (Erotic Contemporary, Ellora's Cave)

www.ingramcontent.com/pod-product-compliance
Lightning Source LLC
Chambersburg PA
CBHW070523130626
46555CB00003B/1315